THE MURDER OF DEVON STONE

Other Books By Marc D. Hasbrouck

Another Word For Murder
Remember You Must Die
Murder On The Street Of Years
Down With The Sun
Stable Affairs
Horse Scents

THE MURDER OF DEVON STONE

MARC DERRY HASBROUCK

THE MURDER OF DEVON STONE

iUniverse books may be ordered through booksellers or by contacting:

iUniverse
1663 Liberty Drive
Bloomington, IN 47403
www.iuniverse.com
844-349-9409

Because of the dynamic nature of the Internet, any web addresses or links contained in this book may have changed since publication and may no longer be valid. The views expressed in this work are solely those of the author and do not necessarily reflect the views of the publisher, and the publisher hereby disclaims any responsibility for them.

Any people depicted in stock imagery provided by Getty Images are models, and such images are being used for illustrative purposes only.
Certain stock imagery © Getty Images.

Interior Image Credit: Gaylin E. Hasbrouck

ISBN: 978-1-6632-6139-7 (sc)
ISBN: 978-1-6632-6140-3 (e)

Library of Congress Control Number: 2024906179

Print information available on the last page.

iUniverse rev. date: 03/20/2024

This book is dedicated to my wife, Gaylin.

Our friendship began when we were fifteen years old and it grew and flourished into something splendiferous from that point on.

A SHORT NOTE FROM THE AUTHOR

Here I go again. Coincidences. Being in the wrong place at the right time. Being in the right place at the wrong time. Or being in the right place at the perfect time. I remember reading somewhere that coincidences are fine in real life, but in fiction they're just bad writing. Fortunately for you, my readers, I obviously do not agree.

I find that writing murder mysteries taking place during the 1950s adds fun to the challenge. No cell phones. No Internet. No telephone answering machines. No Caller I.D. No security cameras. In my last three thrillers, my characters have bounced around from London, to Paris, on to Hong Kong, the streets of New York City, and the hinterlands of New Jersey. Mayhem in all those locales! Devon Stone, my alter ego, stays pretty much close to his hometown, London, in *this* book but his mind with incredible memory via hyperthymesia covers a lot of foreign territory. Although you need not to have read my first thriller *Murder On The Street Of years* to enjoy this one, there is a slight nod to something briefly mentioned there that comes to fruition here.

I had posed the question in my previous thrillers if murder can ever be justified. In *Murder On The Street Of Years* I obviously felt that it could be. Not so with *this* book. The brutal murders that happen within the following pages cannot be justified in any way. Well, okay…maybe one can be.

Bear in mind that this book is a thriller, and the style in which *I* normally write; therefore you can anticipate some silliness accompanied by some snippets of actual history along with the mystery.

So please check your senses of logic and reality at the door as you come in, and embrace your wildest imagination. I let *my* wildest imagination run rampant and, at times, violently so.

Let's begin, shall we?

PART ONE

RETROSPECTIVE

"The truth is rarely pure and never simple."

Oscar Wilde – The Importance of Being Earnest

PROLOGUE

March 24, **1956** – Hampstead, London, England

It was nearing closing time at the Holly Bush but the patrons, many of whom were drunk as lords, weren't in any hurry to leave. The running of the Grand National earlier in the day had left everyone in a giddy mood, especially because of that odd, startling occurrence.

Every time the door opened as someone was exiting, raucous drunken laughter and conversation spilled out into the chilly night air. One by one, or in twos and threes, it was mostly men who ambled in one direction or the other down the winding Holly Mount on the way to their respective homes, still laughing and chattering as they went.

In the shadows a disgruntled man was waiting. Hiding behind a clump of trees and a brick wall. He was a man small in stature, not even reaching five feet in height, and looking to be in his mid to late fifties. He was clean-shaven and had long dark stringy hair hanging over his forehead. A scar ran down the right hand side of his face from his hairline to his chin. He was wearing a dark-colored double-breasted mackintosh fastened with a belt and black trousers. His calf-high boots were covered in dried mud. He slunk further down as two prattling and laughing men passed his hiding place. Neither one was the man for whom he was waiting. He looked back toward the pub to make certain no one else was out and about.

He was getting impatient.

A slight chilly misty rain had started to drizzle, making him even angrier. He was tired. He was hungry. He was cold. He was shivering. Now he was getting wet and he was frustrated.

Thoughts from the turbulent past mingled with those of the uncertain present.

Five minutes later the door to the pub opened once again and the man's intended target stepped out onto the narrow sidewalk.

"Blast!" said the man to himself silently as he pushed back into the shrubbery. His target was not alone. The two men started walking toward him as they chatted and laughed as two good long-time friends would.

They casually passed.

You bastard, he thought, as he glared at his target that, now, was practically within reach.

He then quickly, cautiously, silently stepped out from the shadows and onto the sidewalk, retrieving a Model 34 Beretta from his jacket. He raised his right arm, aiming carefully. The darkness concealed his sinister smirk. He waited until the two men were not walking as closely as they had been upon leaving the Holly Bush. Once, a decade ago, he had been a marksman. He was certain of a kill.

"At long last and once and for all, goodbye Devon Stone," he chuckled silently to himself as he pulled the trigger.

1

Six Months Earlier...

Devon Stone lowered his just fired pistol. He had aimed into the hollowing trunk of an aging pedunculate oak tree. Arriving in the Hampstead Heath shortly after dawn in hopes that there would be no one around at that hour, he was testing the recoil of his latest addition to his collection, a .38 caliber Colt Cobra. He had just turned fifty-one and bought himself a birthday present.

The sun had yet to break the horizon, but its first golden light was just beginning to kiss the top limbs of the tallest trees setting them ablaze with color. It was a brisk late September morning with the temperature around 12°C.

"Hey, mister, are you trying to put that poor old tree out of its misery?" called a giggly voice from far behind him. "Why dontcha pick on someone your *own* size!"

Devon Stone recognized that voice.

He smirked as he turned around.

"Amy, what in blazes are *you* doing out here at the crack of dawn?" he asked.

Amaryllis Cormier, a perky young lady of about twenty-five stood with her hands on her slim hips. Her dark auburn hair was cropped close, in the new pixie style that seemed to be the rage of the younger generation these days. She was wearing dungarees rolled up at the cuffs and a heavy hunter green turtleneck sweater to ward off the autumn chill.

"And you better not have shot my dog, Devon, or I'll wrestle that gun from you and send you off to have a private conversation with Jesus!"

Amaryllis put the tips of her thumb and forefinger together, pressed them to her lips and created a whistle that nearly pierced Devon's eardrums.

Off to the right, Devon heard some rustling in the bushes and a frisky, liver-colored Labrador retriever bounded out toward them. Without fear or hesitation the dog stopped at Devon's side and started sniffing him up and down.

"Good boy, Winston," the young lady said, still giggling. "Watch your crotch, Devon. He's a poker."

Devon Stone laughed and offered the backside of his hand for the dog to sniff before bending down to ruffle Winston's ears. His face was licked as a reward.

"Love your name, boy," he said to the friendly canine. "Are you out here terrorizing the squirrels?"

At the sound of that last word Winston immediately stopped sniffing Devon. He pricked up his ears and looked around frantically.

"Was that reaction a coincidence, Amy, or did he just understand me?"

Amaryllis Cormier laughed and shook her head.

"Oh, Winston is *extremely* smart, Devon. He understands dozens of words and just as many commands. Watch this."

Amy clapped her hands.

"Winston, get the stick!"

The dog took a stance, looking all around him and ran off toward the woods. Less than a minute later he returned with a long branch in his mouth. He ran up to Amy and dropped it right in front of her.

"Bloody hell," laughed Devon.

"Squirrel! Get the squirrel!" Amy squealed excitedly, pointing toward the trees.

Winston ran off, again in the direction of the woods, barking all the way. He stopped at the base of the tree that Devon had just shot, put his front paws up on the trunk and started bouncing and barking loudly. Devon looked up into the branches and saw three squirrels leaping from limb to limb and then jumping onto adjacent trees as a large flock of roosting ravens suddenly took flight. He watched as the just-disturbed birds swooped and called angrily.

Many people associate ravens with death and, to some, they represent bad omens of things to come. Ravens live within the Tower of London, and the local superstition is that if the Tower of London ravens fly away then the Crown will fall and Britain with it.

Amy whistled loudly once again, startling Devon who wasn't prepared for the shrill sound, and Winston came bounding back to them. Devon watched as the birds continued to swoop overhead.

"Did you know, Amy, that a flock of ravens is called an unkindness?" Devon asked, pointing to the birds in flight.

"I did *not* know that, Devon…but I know that you're a writer and *you* know stupid shit like that."

Devon Stone laughed.

Amaryllis Cormier had been an American student coming to England to study Classic Literature at Cambridge University following the war. But she found it to be rather restrictive toward woman so she soon dropped out after the first year. She now worked in the West End as the store manager at The Poisoned Quill, the bookshop owned by Devon's friend, Lydia Hyui.

Her parents back in the States owned a popular florist shop and garden center, Petal Pushers, in affluent Millburn, New Jersey. She had three older sisters: Rose, Lily, and Dahlia…and a younger brother named Aster. Although it was totally coincidental but completely true, her mother's first name was Fern and her father's first name was Gardener.

"I've got to hurry back and get Winston home. I'll probably be late for work. I've got to open the shop. Lydia is still in Hong Kong visiting with her brother again, so I don't fear getting admonished," Amy giggled once again. "By the way, how's your new publisher, Devon? Has *he* killed anyone lately?"

Devon's previous long-time publisher, James Flynn, had murdered Samuel Fleck, a hack writer, the year before. When confronted with the truth by both Devon and the dead writer's son, Flynn committed suicide by leaping from his office window to the London streets ten floors below.

Devon Stone laughed, shaking his head.

"You Americans can be so blunt at times."

Amaryllis Cormier chuckled and shrugged her shoulders.

"He *is* going to take some getting used to," Devon answered her question. "Probably a *lot* of time getting used to, for that matter. He's much younger than Flynn, and I find him to be a bit too conservative for my tastes at the moment…and a bit on the prissy side. Like with your dog Winston there, the guy and I are going through that tail sniffing stage checking each other out. I haven't found out yet if that's his real name or he made it up to sound refined and sophisticated."

"And that name is?"

Devon cleared his throat.

"Are you ready for this one? Christian de Lindsay."

"Dollars to donuts, it's made up. Sounds like a fop name to me, doesn't it? Break him in easy, Devon. Don't shock the poor guy too much with your violent murders. The fictitious ones, I mean." And she winked at Devon.

What did she mean by that, Devon thought. *She doesn't have a clue about my past history.*

"Gotta run, Devon," Amy said as she whistled for Winston once more. "Not that you're interested or anything, but I think Lydia is getting pretty chummy with that Jeremy Fleck guy down there in Hong Kong. Didn't you and my boss have a thing going there for a while?"

"What did I just say about you Americans being blunt? Amy, setting the record straight, Lydia and I are just…casual friends."

Amy laughed.

"Yeah, right. Pajama parties without the pajamas."

"Good bye, Amy…oh, and goodbye to you, too, Winston! Now I've got a book to finish."

Devon Stone shook his head and laughed as he watched the two run off, Winston barking all the way.

As he meandered across the Heath the ravens silently returned to their roost in the tall oak.

2

The sun was just beginning to break through the early morning misty clouds as Richard Fleming stood, naked, out his balcony and stared up at the Acropolis a few blocks away. It would soon be another hot day. He flicked his cigarette butt down onto the street below. He didn't care about exposing his nakedness. He was proud of his lean, tan and toned body. He pushed his dark blond hair back off his forehead and yawned.

"Bugger," he muttered to himself as he turned to go inside to answer his ringing telephone.

He nonchalantly scratched his balls as he picked up the receiver.

"Yeah, what?" he answered with a lazy sigh. Only one person on the entire planet who would be calling knew where he was now and how to reach him.

"Playtime's over for a while," came the familiar voice. "We need to solve a slight problem. Nothing major…for now. But I'm certain you can handle it. Get back to London quickly and just as quickly you can get right back to your whoring there in Athens. Better bring your umbrella this time. I know how you just hate to get…wet."

"Fuck off," Richard Fleming said, but then they both laughed. "I'll call ya as soon as I get in town."

And the phone call ended abruptly.

He put the receiver back in the cradle and looked down at the snoring woman in his rumpled bed. With a swift jerk he pulled the covers off the naked dark-haired beauty and swatted her on her butt.

"Hey, Sophia, time to get out, ducky!"

The woman groaned and rolled over slowly.

"My name ain't Sophia, handsome," she said in a thick Greek accent. She stretched and yawned as her eyes fluttered and then opened.

"I don't give a flyin' fuck whatever the hell it is, just get your sweet arse outta that bed and back to the streets where you belong."

He was standing right next to her as she reached up her hand.

"Oooh, can't I have just one more piece of *that*?" she asked as she took hold of his penis. "You're delicious, honey." He was starting to get erect.

He backed away and she released her grip.

"When I get back in town, maybe. Then again, maybe not. Move it!"

After she had hurriedly dressed and left, Richard Fleming walked into his bathroom.

He was now fully erect. He stroked himself a few times but decided that he really didn't want to complete the act. The thought of what he might be going to do in London thrilled him in a totally different way.

He stared at himself in the large mirror. He always liked what he saw. Dark blond hair, perfectly trimmed. Bold blue eyes that had mesmerized countless women. And, at twenty-seven, an exceptional specimen of masculinity. All ego aside.

The bitch was right, he thought. *I am* handsome.

He ran his right hand across his smooth, defined chest, caressing his pectorals. He toyed with one of his rigid nipples and smiled.

His nipples were the center point for two tattoos. Of his many tattoos, on his chest were the prominent tattoos of which he was most proud. Side-by-side Swastikas.

3

Hampstead Heath is a hilly, grassy public space sitting atop a sandy ridge and is one of the highest points in London. It covers seven hundred and ninety acres containing ponds, ancient woodlands, walking trails, a lido, and playgrounds. It was here, a few years earlier that had been the place where, once and for all, the last of the Nazi sympathizers who had been killing the Soviet Night Witches had met her demise. Devon was content that this nasty piece of business was now far behind him.

But he was mistaken in a manner of speaking. A different, albeit violent part of his past was soon to catch up with him. Unfinished business lay ahead.

Devon Stone walked casually out of the Heath and hiked the short distance to his row house on Carlingford Road. A small flock of homing pigeons swooped silently low overhead as he climbed his front steps. He knew exactly where the birds would come in for a landing. He picked up the morning newspaper from his doorstep and went in.

After fixing himself a steaming cup of coffee, he grabbed the newspaper and climbed the three floors to his rooftop garden. The row houses, being attached side by side, shared a low wall between the adjacent houses. Devon's neighbor was on his own rooftop tending to the just-landed flock of birds.

"Good morning, Chester!" Devon called out, waving his hand as he did so.

A female hand popped up from a chair that had been hidden from view by the wall and waved a salutation. The chair's back was facing Devon and his wall.

"And good morning to you, *too*, Devon. Gorgeous day, what?" called out Chester's lady friend.

"Oh, good morning to you, too, Fiona," Devon answered. "I didn't see you there. Yes, it is a lovely morning. A nice day ahead no doubt."

Fiona Thayer had been in MI5 and Devon's neighbor, Chester Davenport, had been MI6 during World War II, now being its retired Chief. Fiona had been one of Devon's "accomplices" in routing out the killers of some of the Soviet Night Witches. Fiona had been brutally attacked and left for dead at one point but managed to survive and went through an extensive recovery period. Physically and emotionally. She looked none the worse for wear. In fact, she looked and acted years younger than she actually was, somewhere in her early seventies.

For sensitive security reasons, details of MI6 operations and its personnel seldom appeared in the British press, consequently only a select few of Devon's friends knew of Chester and Fiona's backgrounds.

By the time Devon Stone had downed his second cup of coffee and finished reading the morning paper, Richard Fleming had boarded his airplane at Hassani Airport, recently renamed Athenai International Airport, in Athens and settled in for the flight to London. His aircraft, a Vickers Viscount, was the first turboprop-powered airliner. The British European Airways craft was well received by its passengers and Richard Fleming enjoyed the panoramic window view as the plane took off out over the sparkling Ionian Sea. After winking and smiling flirtatiously at the pretty blonde stewardess, he leaned back in his seat and eagerly anticipated his upcoming assignment.

Richard Fleming was an assassin.
Pure and simple.

The product of a turbulent, unhappy family life, his father had been killed during World War II and he was left with a verbally and physically abusive mother. Without compunction, at the age of fifteen he murdered his mother, making it look like suicide by hanging her from the rafters in their garage and writing a fake suicide note. He turned to petty crimes at first, then murder…and eventually murder for hire as his reputation amongst the underworld spread. With his youthful good looks, precision, and stealth, he never came under suspicion by the authorities for any of his crimes, no matter in which country they had been committed. Almost always he left only one untraceable, yet very distinctive signature clue behind at a majority of his killings. His lethal endeavors proved to be quite lucrative by the time he reached his current age. He owned a large apartment in both London and Athens and possessed the latest Maserati in each locale.

He was one of the best and he knew it. He never asked questions and couldn't care less about his intended victims, male or female. He had no compassion whatsoever as he performed his various assignments. He simply enjoyed watching others die by his hand.

His weapon of choice was a Fairbairn-Sykes fighting knife, a double-edged weapon resembling a poignard. These fighting knives, originally developed in Shanghai in 1941, were issued to British Commandos during the war and Fleming's weapon had once belonged to his father. The weapon was best used for thrusting but can also be utilized for inflicting deadly slash cuts. It was also easily concealed.

But he would use a different weapon for this particular assignment. A weapon of his own design. And one that was so innocuous that there was no need for it to be concealed.

———⫸◉⫷———

Devon Stone sat at his typewriter self-editing chapter twenty-two of his latest book, the chapter that he had written last night. He was correcting the few careless mistakes made because of a few too many gin and tonics before calling it a night. He chuckled to himself at the title, *I Dream Of Death*, about a murderous fraudulent clairvoyant. The idea had come to him after attending a screening of the old 1945 film *Blithe Spirit* by Noel Coward. But instead of describing his murderess as someone looking and acting like the delightful Margaret Rutherford in the film, he created a ravishing flame-haired beauty that would seduce very wealthy and foolhardy male believers in the afterlife and, therefore, effortlessly and ruthlessly, "escort" them *to* that afterlife. Halfway through his first draft, he wasn't sure yet if he would have the conniving murderess, Madame Cyrenne, portend her own demise.

Words were flowing like gutters after the deluge when he was interrupted by his telephone ringing. He kept typing long enough to punctuate the last sentence, and just before his mystic murderess could send her latest victim to the great beyond with a martini laced with strychnine.

He picked up after the third ring of the phone, answered, and then heard a familiar voice.

"Stone, my good man, how in blazes have you been?"

The voice belonged to Clovis James, theater critic for *The*

Guardian. He was also one of Devon's very close friends and one of the brave group secretly bringing about the end to all the nefarious miscreants killing the Night Witches. Clovis had ended the life of the dreadful actor Gregory Montgomery on Bonfire Night back in 1952. Gregory Montgomery had been the one that murdered Clovis's beloved aunt, Mildred Wallace. Clovis had been unable to pronounce the name Mildred as a young child and therefore had called her Aunt Min. Because of that and being that she stood slightly over 5' she became lovingly known by all her friends as Little Min.

"Well, Clovis! How nice to hear your voice again. Sorry I've been a bit out of touch. Have you killed off any dreadful performances lately? Metaphorically speaking, that is."

They both laughed. Clovis James was known amongst the London theater world as being a severe critic. Brutal with his scathing, albeit accurate reviews.

"To be honest, I had a marvelous time again at *Kismet* at the Stoll Theatre a couple nights ago. I say *again*, because it's the third time I've seen it. Wonderful show and how can you beat that Borodin music? I took a fellow critic friend, an *art* critic, with me. His wife didn't want to see it for some reason and I always get house seats for every performance."

"I've not seen it, Clovis," answered Devon. "You know my aversion to musicals."

"Yes, I'm well aware of that. But it may have been *truly* kismet that my friend then invited me to attend an opening at an art gallery for last evening."

"Oh?"

"Yes, well then," answered Clovis James. "You may or may not know that my sweet Aunt Min harbored a belief that her husband had met his end *not* by accident. Unfortunately she carried that thought to the grave. This exhibition that I attended last evening was a retrospective of wartime photography by a rather well known photographer by the name of Drew Devereaux."

"Sorry, old chap. I may be a writer who knows a lot of things, but I've not heard of him."

"Wrong gender, Devon. Wrong gender. Drew Devereaux is female and an exceptionally talented one at that. I want you to come to that gallery with me…either later this afternoon or tomorrow, if possible. At your convenience, of course. There is one photo in particular that I'd like you to see. My late Uncle Alistair, Aunt Min's husband, happens to be in it. But there is another person in that photo that might lead me to believe that my aunt was correct."

"Seriously?"

"Yes, seriously, Devon. There is the possibility, remote, as it may seem, that my uncle was, indeed, murdered. And if so, you know who the killer was. Or is."

4

Richard Fleming drew back the curtains in the living room of his London apartment letting the late afternoon glow of sunlight warm up the room. In the distance he could see the Tower of London and parts of the Tower Bridge, which spanned the Thames. The teakettle that he had put on the stove after he first arrived thirty minutes earlier began to whistle. He poured his Earl Grey into a cup, topping it off with a healthy splash of Scotch.

He stood by the window, watching the traffic go by five flights below, while sipping his tea. He was patiently waiting for his telephone to ring.

He didn't have to wait long.

⊱⋅⊰

Drew Devereaux began her interest in photography before she reached five years of age. Borrowing her mother's little camera, a Kodak No. 2 Brownie Model E, she first started photographing her dog Ambrose, a Boston terrier, and then progressing to landscapes around her yard. At that age, she was not permitted to leave her property unattended. The older she got, the better the cameras she was given with which to play. And the further she was permitted to roam. By the time she was in her early teens she was processing her own film and enlarging her own prints in the darkroom her father had built for her in their basement.

Following her graduation from university, majoring in Photo Journalism, and bucking the prejudice of women opening their own businesses, she opened her own commercial photography studio concentrating on architectural and industrial photography.

In 1942, after much cajoling of the editors of the *London Times*, she became one of the first female war correspondents and, ultimately, one of the first female journalists to bravely venture into combat zones. Even in the most brutal of environments, she was equipped with five cameras, twenty-two lenses of various lengths, five developing tanks, processing chemicals, and over three thousand flashbulbs. Her results were published in the press around the globe, even earning an award winning cover photograph on *LIFE Magazine* in the United States.

Now, at the age of forty, she couldn't believe that she was actually having an installation of her works at the prestigious Whitechapel Art Gallery, a facility dating back to 1901.

She and the curator worked very closely in selecting the appropriate prints to be shown. Some of the photos could be upsetting with their graphic depiction of war's destructive powers. She also wanted to show the human aspect of bravery along with suffering. She had risked her life to capture the essence of the brutal war and had actually been wounded more than once. Above all, she didn't want to sugar coat the exhibition in any way.

The exhibit at Whitechapel would be a dramatic one, startling at times in its sheer horror of war.

But she had no way of knowing what deadly events would be set in motion because of it.

Fleming hung up following his awaited call and shrugged his shoulders. He knew why his caller couldn't have done the job himself, although he, too, was a ruthless, brutal killer. Sometimes appearances can alert the intended victim.

This would be a swift and easy kill. And one that would put an easy thousand pounds into his bank account. The kill would also be convenient. The victim-to-be had his business on Whitechapel High Street, within walking distance of where Fleming stood at the moment.

Early the next afternoon, Richard Fleming strolled into *Bet's On!*, a bookmaker, and one with a bit of a shady history. There were no races today. No current games on which to bet. So the proprietor was alone probably doing paperwork, as Fleming knew he would be.

Andy Potts sat at a desk smoking an old pipe, filling the air with the aroma of Peterson Irish Flake. He was in his late 50s, balding, and at least fifty pounds overweight. He stood up as Fleming entered the building.

"Good afternoon, chappy," called out Andy Potts, the man who would *not* be enjoying his evening tea. "Expecting rain are, ya?" he laughed as he saw the unopened umbrella that Fleming was holding.

"Well, one never knows when one might need it here in London," Fleming answered with nary a smile.

Potts smiled and exhaled a whiff of that sweet smelling smoke.

Fleming looked around to make certain the shop was, indeed, empty. He was starting to get aroused. Killing always gave him a sturdy erection. There had actually been times when he ejaculated as he sent his latest victim to their death.

"I believe you may have cheated someone recently, Mr. Potts," he said, now with a sneer beginning to cross his face. "Someone who doesn't like to be cheated."

The older man's smile disappeared and he looked confused.

"What the bloody hell are you talking about? How do you know my name, lad?" he asked nervously.

"I've come to make good on that bet, you oily bastard. Evidently my friend just can't *stand* being cheated. He simply can't be arsed by someone like you, so he sent me."

Fleming took a step toward his victim, frightening the man. The assassin could feel his erection growing stronger.

"You nicked him more than a few quid, ya did, you old sot," sneered Fleming.

"Get out!" demanded Andy Potts. "Get out of my fucking shop! I'll alert the Bobbies. Get out!" and he approached Richard Fleming with fists raised.

Wrong move.

Richard Fleming made another step toward the angered man and Potts turned around heading toward his telephone.

Another wrong move.

Richard Fleming lunged forward, stabbing the man in the back with the tip of his umbrella.

"What the fuck! What did you just do?" screamed Potts as he reached around clutching at his back.

"I just unlocked the doorway to Hell, old man, and you're about to step through."

The umbrella had a built-in needle, which injected mercury into Potts's back. He stopped in his tracks. A strange and unpleasant sensation began to surge through his body. He felt immediate tingling in his hands as they went numb, a fever quickly broke out and his breathing became so rapid he thought he was having a heart attack. He clutched at his chest as he fell to the floor.

"What's the matter, old chap?" laughed Fleming as he bent down looking into the gasping man's eyes. "Aw, not feeling so well? I believe that's called tachycardia. Don't worry, though, it'll stop soon. But then, you'll never know it."

Richard Fleming came close to the point of ejaculation, but

held his breath, keeping his emotions in check as he stood back and watched the man die on the floor.

"Debt paid in full," the assassin said aloud as he kicked the dead body viciously in the side of the head.

The telephone started ringing but Fleming simply lifted the receiver out of the cradle and laid it back down onto the desk.

He casually walked to the front door, turning out the lights as he did so. He switched the little sign hanging at the front window from OPEN to CLOSED.

He exited the building into brilliant sunshine and slowly walked up Whitechapel High Street looking for a coffee shop, if there was one. He whistled a jaunty tune as he strolled, with the umbrella casually resting atop his shoulder.

He felt like Gene Kelly in *Singing In The Rain*.

5

Clovis James was already at the Whitechapel Art Gallery when Devon Stone walked in. There were a couple other people in the gallery, slowly ambling from one print to the next, stopping for a short gaze, then moving along. Devon, too, stopped from photo to photo before sidling up to his friend. He had noticed that all of the prints had specific titles as to the locale where they were photographed, and the appropriate dates when the photo had been taken.

"Actually," Devon said without a greeting, "I *have* seen some of these photographs before in various publications over the years. I just never paid much attention, or questioned about their creator."

"Hello, Stone," said Clovis, "Thanks for coming. I'll bet you probably assumed all the pictures were shot by a man...or men, didn't you?"

"You're probably right, Clovis. I'm now ashamed to admit my misogyny."

"Oh, bosh!" answered the drama critic laughing. "You don't have a misogynistic bone in your body. You were just being ignorant."

The two men looked at one another and broke out laughing.

"The photo in question, Stone, is around that corner down there. As I mentioned to you on the phone, Aunt Min was convinced that my uncle's death was murder, not an accident as reported in all the papers."

"I remember the situation, Clovis."

"Jesus! You remember *everything*, Stone!" chuckled Clovis James.

"Supposedly he tripped on some rubble from a bombed out building in the street and fell in front of a speeding army vehicle of some sort, or something like that, Right?" asked Devon Stone.

"You have the scenario correct. *But.* Yes, it was an army vehicle. I believe it was a Humber Heavy Utility Car. It was a nasty hit. Uncle Alistair suffered multiple internal injuries and remained alert and barely lucid enough until Aunt Min arrived at hospital. Feisty as she was, she insisted upon seeing her husband immediately. He groggily told her he was certain he was pushed. And he mentioned something about a very small man. He expired before he could say anything else. The authorities were too busy fighting a war to pursue it any further. His accusation was, therefore, ignored and forgotten."

The two men walked along through the gallery and came to a stop in front of the photograph that had grabbed the attention of the drama critic.

They both stared at the large, framed 36" X 45" black and white print.

"Bloody hell!" gasped Devon Stone.

Richard Fleming hadn't found a coffee shop yet along the street, so he decided to go into an intriguing looking art gallery. The building was an old, yellow stone-fronted one with absolutely no windows. The name, Whitechapel Art Gallery, was carved into the smooth façade over the entryway, which were two massive wooden doors that were painted a stark black. Above that rested a half-circle window with metal bars. Fleming thought that it looked more like a prison, but he had found it interesting enough to stop and look at it. There were framed posters on either side of the entryway

22

advertising the current exhibits, one of which was *World War II: A Retrospective In Focus*. He had been a teenager when the war ended but it still fascinated him. His unloving father had been killed during it and Fleming's favorite weapon was from that conflict. Although he was patriotic and loved his Queen and country, inwardly he still regretted that Hitler was unable to successfully complete his Final Solution.

He pulled open one of the heavy doors and stepped inside. The hardwood floors creaked as he started perusing the gallery. *Someone must be burning an incense*, he thought. It smelled of sandalwood.

He casually meandered from photo to photo.

"Expecting rain, young man?" laughed an older woman who was also walking around the gallery.

Richard Fleming glanced down at his umbrella and chuckled, shrugging his shoulders.

"We're in London, right?" he answered with a broad smile. "Doesn't it rain like clockwork here every afternoon?"

"Seems that way," answered the woman as she moved along. They exchanged smiles.

I just hate to get…wet, he snickered to himself.

Fleming rounded a corner and watched as two men were in animated conversation in front of one of the larger prints. He continued to move slowly from one photo to the next, still keeping an eye on those two men.

What intrigues them so much, he thought to himself. *Obviously something of interest to them both.*

He moved a bit closer and was able to pick up a smattering of their conversation.

"Oh, that's definitely him," said the taller of the two men. "No doubt."

"But, surely he's long dead by now, after what you did to him," said the other man.

"I want to see if I can contact the photographer. Perhaps she has other negatives of this scenario. Look at that date. Isn't that when your uncle had his accident?"

"I'm sure the curator here can get us in touch with Miss Devereaux," said the other man.

Richard Fleming stood back and pretended to show interest in a nearby print as he watched out of the corner of his eye as the men walked to the front of the gallery. He waited until they had rounded the corner and were out of view. He nonchalantly approached the large print and looked at it.

His mouth dropped open.

"Uh, oh," he said aloud.

6

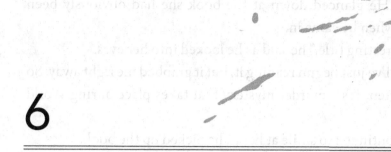

It had been a slow day at The Poisoned Quill so Amaryllis Cormier was finally going to catch up on the one Devon Stone book she had not yet read. She picked up a signed copy of *Wheels Within Wheels* and started to read. It was a World War II espionage thriller regarding the Nazi's Enigma Machine. A voracious reader, she had just finished Patricia Highsmith's *The Talented Mr. Ripley* and loved it. She was most perplexed by the psyche of a con man and a killer who apparently had no conscience whatsoever.

Goodness, how can someone like that ever live with themselves, she thought to herself.

Little did she know that, by sheer happenstance, she would soon find out.

Her reading was interrupted by the little bell over the front door indicating that she had a potential customer entering the shop. She put the book down on the counter as she watched him walk around.

Well, isn't he a little dreamboat, she thought as she continued to stare at the handsome young man. The young man smiled at her and nodded as he started wandering through the aisles.

She's a little bobby-dazzler, he thought to himself as he continued to steal some quick glances at her.

He slowly made his way up to the counter where Amy was

smiling. He glanced down at the book she had obviously been reading when he came in.

"Interesting title," he said as he looked into her eyes.

"Oh, I've just begun reading it, but it grabbed me right away. So well written. It's a murder mystery that takes place during World War II."

He continued to smile at her as he picked up the book.

"That war fascinates me and I always love a good murder... mystery," said Richard Fleming.

The assassin had a few hours to kill, no pun intended, before he would receive his anticipated phone call. Being that it was a beautiful afternoon, he decided to just roam around the city for a while and ended up in the West End. He was eager to impart his interesting trip to the art gallery with his current sometimes boss.

"Expecting rain, are we?" laughed Amaryllis Cormier as she spied the man's umbrella. "I know the London weather can be iffy, but it's gorgeous out there today. So far, anyway."

"Ah, a Yank, are ya?" chuckled Richard Fleming, ignoring the umbrella comment.

"You can tell?" giggled Amy as she fluttered her eyes.

They were both flirting.

Fleming glanced, again, at the book that Amy had been reading.

"I may have to give this one a try. I read on occasion, when I get the chance. Life keeps me busy," he said as he slowly turned the book over to look at the back.

He stared at the photo of Devon Stone on the back cover, cocked his head, and got a quizzical look on his face.

Why does he look familiar to me, he thought.

Amaryllis Cormier notice his expression.

"Why that look? Do you know this author?" she asked.

"No...no, I certainly don't know him. He just looks familiar for some reason. Perhaps I may have seen some other of his books somewhere, that's all."

"Well, he's a really swell guy, as well as a brilliant writer."

Richard Fleming cocked his head.

"You know him?" he asked, tilting his head to one side.

"Oh, yeah! Well, I mean, I've known him for only a short time but he and my boss are...shall we say, close."

"Interesting. Let me buy a copy of that book. This could be the start of something. I mean...like reading *all* of his books if they're as good as you say."

"That's swell, mister....?"

"Just call me Joe. Just plain Joe," he said with a wink.

She coyly smiled back at him.

This guy is so darn cute, she thought to herself.

"And *your* name, missy?" he asked.

"My name is Amaryllis, but you can call me Amy. Just plain Amy," she giggled.

"Oh, no," he said with a broad smile. "You're too beautiful to be just plain anything."

She blushed.

He winked.

And he handed her a £20 note.

She rang up the sale, handed his change back to him, and placed the book into a paper bag with the store's logo on it. Richard Fleming glanced at it and snickered.

"The name of this shop is what made me stop in and take a look," he said as he took the bag from Amy, making sure to slightly touch her hand gently as he did so. "Maybe I'll be back," he said as he winked at her once again, this time with a more flirtatious smile and an arched eyebrow.

"I'd like that 'just plain Joe'," she smiled back. "I'd love to know how you liked the book."

"Perhaps we can discuss it over coffee sometime. You know, like a book report at school," and he laughed.

The bell to the shop rang as another customer entered.

"See you around, sweet pea," Richard Fleming said, oozing charm with a seductive glint in his eyes.

He turned around, giving Amy a quick little two-finger salute as he passed the potential customer and exited out into the street.

Amy sighed and smiled.

"Oh, my!" she said out loud.

7

The awaited phone call came.

Richard Fleming had just finished reading chapter three in *Wheels Within Wheels* and was on his second Scotch on the rocks.

"Was it a rainy day on Whitechapel High Street?" asked his caller as soon as Fleming had answered.

"Oh, it was a real killer," laughed the assassin.

"Good. Always glad to hear. That's why you're the fuckin' best there is. Don't get your ass back to Athens just yet, though. I think there just might be more some rain in the forecast."

"I was gonna stick around here for a while anyway," answered Fleming. "Nothing pressing for me back in Greece at the moment."

There was a pause and a silence. Richard Fleming wasn't sure how to approach what he had seen in the art gallery earlier in the afternoon.

He cleared his throat.

"I know that you don't usually go to any art galleries or museums or shit places like that…but you just might want to stop by the Whitechapel Gallery. It's just a couple blocks away from where that…ahh…rain storm was this afternoon."

"Oh, yeah? Why?"

"It's a show with photographs. Photographs back to World War II. And…uh…well…you're *in* one of them."

Amaryllis Cormier was locking up the bookshop for the day. She had tried to get back reading Devon's book but her mind kept wandering. She couldn't stop thinking about that great looking guy with the beautiful blue eyes. She had dated a few young gentlemen here in London but none interesting enough or held her attention long enough to progress to the second or third date.

But this guy, she thought, *might be different.*

She just didn't know how different *this* guy could be.

"Oh, yeah? What was the picture that I'm in?"

"Hard to describe, really," answered Richard Fleming. "It looks like a bombed out building is in the back ground, sorta out of focus. And maybe some flames, I think. A couple guys seem to be running...like toward the camera, I guess, and there's a shitload of rubble and crap in the street they're trying to cross."

"I just might have to stop by and take a gander. Maybe I'm famous, eh?" and the man laughed. "Me ugly puss hanging in a fucking art gallery."

Richard Fleming paused.

"Ahh, well...you might want to be a bit careful if you do," said Fleming, not knowing how tactfully he must approach his next statement. "It's not as though you can disguise yourself that easily."

"What the *fuck* do ya mean by that?" the man exploded.

"What I mean is, that there were two guys looking at that photograph and, from what I picked up overhearing their conversation, they recognized you."

"Oh?"

"Yes, and evidently they think that you must be long dead because of what one of the men did to you."

Long silence.

Richard Fleming began to get nervous.

"Fuck!" finally screamed the man into the phone. "Fuck, fuck, holy fuck! I was hoping *he* was dead by now! He *should* be, anyway."

"Who?"

"Daniel Stein!"

Devon Stone is a pen name. Only a select few know that the name that appears on his passport is Daniel Stein, his given name. While it was never mentioned anywhere in his literary biography, Devon, ne Daniel, worked for Britain's Naval Intelligence Division up to and through World War II. This is how he met his two good current friends, Fiona Thayer and Chester Davenport, of MI5 and MI6.

"Oh," Fleming responded, sounding disappointed. "Maybe it's *not* who I thought he was after all."

"Why? Who's that?"

"Well, I happened to buy a book after that little…ah…rainstorm this afternoon and the author's picture was on the back cover. He looked vaguely familiar and I thought it might have been one of those guys at the gallery. Maybe I'm mistaken after all. Did you ever read any books by a…" and he had to glance at the author's name again…"Devon Stone?"

"Ha!" laughed the man, "I don't read no books. I ain't read a book since I ran away from reformatory at fifteen!"

"Well, then…" stammered Richard Fleming.

"Yeah, I'll get over to that place. What is it? Where is it?"

"Whitechapel Art Gallery. On Whitechapel High Street. Looks like a prison, but don't be put off by appearances."

"Appearances? Is that another low crack about me?"

"No! Jesus, no. I didn't mean anything like that. Don't be so fucking sensitive."

31

The man laughed.

"I was pulling your leg. Maybe I'll ask Snow White to go with me!"

And the man, Darrin Rand, ended the call with maniacal laughter.

Darrin Rand was born with the genetic disorder called achondroplasia whose primary feature is dwarfism.

Richard Fleming put the receiver back in its cradle and sat back thinking.

"Daniel Stein," he said aloud. "Devon Stone."

Strange coincidence, though, he thought, *same initials. D. S.*

"Devon Stone. Daniel Stein. Stone. Stein. Stein. Stone."

He stopped thinking and abruptly sat up straight.

"Hmmm, interesting", he said again out loud. "Could it be? Could *he* be? Stein is German for stone!"

8

Devon Stone and Clovis James sat talking in a quiet corner at The Holly Bush. They had agreed to meet there several hours after visiting the art gallery.

"The date on that photograph was December twenty-nine," said Devon after taking a long slow sip of his gin and tonic. "1940. That was during the Blitz and that particular bombing, on that particular day, started the Second Great Fire of London."

"Jesus Christ, Stone. Your memory scares the hell out of me."

Devon chuckled and shrugged his shoulders.

"Sorry, old chap. I can't help it. Sometimes it scares the hell out of *me* as well."

"I'll have to check back and see. That may or may not be the day that my Uncle Alistair died…or was killed. But it certainly seems to be pointing in that direction."

Clovis James took a long slow slug of his lukewarm but frothy topped pint of Guinness.

"That curator was certainly obliging," Clovis said as he licked a bit of foam from his lips. "I'll call this Miss Devereaux and see if I can set up an appointment. We need to follow through on this, Stone, and perhaps solve the mystery of which Aunt Min was sure."

"I never knew your uncle, of course. Unfortunately our paths never crossed. But I was certainly extremely fond of Little Min. She was a brave lady to the end. And she could hold her own against me in our respective gin drinking habits. Her 'extra dry' martinis made me laugh. I miss her greatly. But now, as for that bastard Rand, I had him in my crosshairs long before he encountered your uncle. When your aunt said 'little man' I had no idea exactly *how* little she or your uncle meant. And, needless to say, I'm gobsmacked to discover, now, who that 'little man' *was* and what he may have done."

During World War II Devon Stone...then Daniel Stein... was an agent, part of *Churchill's Secret Army*, officially known as Special Operations Executive (SOE). He was a spy. It was a perilous undertaking, to say the least. The tasks of the agents were many. And, at times, deadly. They gathered intelligence, carried out acts of sabotage and being cognizant constantly of double (and possible) triple agents possibly among their midst. Although he was not part of the cryptography teams of Betchley Park who eventually broke the Enigma code, he fictionalized their endeavors and turned it into the best selling thriller that Amaryllis Cormier...and Richard Fleming...were now reading.

Darrin Rand was given the code name "Country Mouse", not only because of his diminutive stature, but also because of his being from Somerset, one of the most rural counties in England. He had had a troubled youth, committing petty crimes, being disruptive in school after being taunted and teased because of his condition, and eventually ending up in the infamous Akbar Reformatory in Heswall, Cheshire. The school offered no respite from his taunting and harassment, and was submitted to severe and sometimes painful punishments for his heinous behavior. Ironically, his background was somewhat similar to the world-class assassin, Richard Fleming, which he now hires on occasion.

In spite of his violent behaviorisms, or perhaps *because* of them, he was recruited by the SOE. Assassinations were not unheard of and because of his stature he could hide himself in the most unexpected of places. But he had concealed one important and dangerous aspect of his personality from his countrymen. His sexual appetite was gargantuan, and he had a male member that belied his short height despite the fact that it was visually startling. He was a spy, an assassin, a thief, a liar, and a rapist.

"You don't suppose that dreadful little man is still alive, do you, Stone?" asked Clovis James as he signaled the barman for another pint.

"I certainly hope not," answered Devon Stone, downing his third gin and tonic and also signaling for a refill. "I know that he ended up in one institution after the other after I got finished with him leaving him scarred, physically as well as mentally. I had heard rumors that he was brutally murdered by another inmate, but that was never corroborated and I never followed up. I was done with him. And done with that aspect of my life. I moved on."

"Well done, Stone. Now just help *me* solve this last mystery surrounding the bloody bloke and we *both* can move on. You have many more books to write and I have many more reputations to bring to a screeching halt in the West End."

They both laughed hysterically and toasted to each other.

⎯⎯⎯⎯⎯►◆◄⎯⎯⎯⎯⎯

Amaryllis Cormier didn't want to stop reading *Wheels Within Wheels* she was enjoying it so much, but her eyes were getting heavy and Winston kept nudging her knee indicating that he was ready for his pre-bedtime walk. His beautiful brown eyes stared into hers. He was sending a strong message and she understood. The several cups of Chamomile tea that she had drunk within the past hour added to her drowsiness, but she grabbed Winston's leash and they went out into the chilly night air. As Winston sniffed around looking for the appropriate spot to do his business, Amy looked up into the clear, starry night. The moon was nearly full and it sort of made her feel romantic and just a bit wistful.

I wonder if 'just plain Joe' is looking up at the moon, too, she thought. *Gee, I sure hope he comes back to the store sometime soon.*

Just plain Joe was, indeed, thinking about Amaryllis Cormier at the moment. But romance didn't figure into the equation.

9

Early afternoon two days later and Devon's typing was interrupted by the telephone.

"Blast!" he said. He was right in the middle of a grisly murder being committed by that deadly clairvoyant in his latest book, and nearly at the end when she is discovered as a fraud and a murderess.

"Hope I haven't interrupted anything too pressing, Stone," said Clovis James sarcastically. "No female companionship over there or anything like today?"

"Sorry to disappoint you, James," Devon responded. "Just me, a typewriter, and only about ten thousand words to go."

"I was finally able to contact Devereaux's studio. Well, her assistant, anyway. Drew Devereaux is currently in Paris preparing for another show, but she'll be returning to her studio tomorrow. Her assistant…Frances, I think she said was her name…penciled us in for a brief meeting around 3 P.M."

"That's fine. Maybe the meeting won't be so brief, but that's fine."

"You might want to come prepared with a gun, Stone. One never knows. Bring one for me, too, while you're at it."

"What the bloody hell does *that* mean?"

"Her studio is on Duval Street."

Silence from Devon Stone.

"Are you serious?" he finally answered.

"Serious as a slit throat, Stone. Seriously."

Duval Street, renamed from Dorset Street in 1904, was once known as "the worst street in London". In November of 1888 it was the scene of the brutal murder of Mary Jane Kelly committed by a person who eventually became known as Jack The Ripper. It was that year, 1888, that a German psychiatrist coined the word *psychopath* from the German word psychopastiche, literally meaning suffering soul. The "suffering soul", that infamous killer (who was never caught) committed several more such murders, and Bobbies would only patrol down the street in pairs. Prostitution was rampant, razor-slashing hoodlums roamed the street terrorizing the populace, and yet there were pubs every few yards.

Following its renaming, many buildings were demolished and the area went through a major redevelopment and a thorough cleansing of its reputation. Small storefront businesses began to flourish.

At 2:56 the following afternoon, their taxicab came to a stop in front of 4901 Duval Street.

Devon Stone and Clovis James looked through the car window and raised their eyebrows.

"This can't be right...can it?" asked Clovis James.

"That's it, buddy," answered the cabbie. "Aren't no other place around with that number."

The storefront was plain, with boarded up windows, no signage stating a business of any kind, and looking rather drab. Just the numbers 4901 in black block letters stenciled across the front of a dingy door.

The two men reluctantly got out of the car, paid the cabbie and bid him farewell. His tires practically screeched as he then sped away. There were a few other people walking up and down

THE MURDER OF DEVON STONE

the sidewalks on both sides of the street. What appeared to be a boutique of some sort was next door, there must have been a bakery nearby because of the enticing aroma wafting through the air, and there was a pub directly across the street seemingly doing a brisk business.

Devon Stone looked all around the doorframe and finally found a small button, obviously to push a doorbell. He did so. And they both waited.

A few minutes later they could hear the door being unlocked. It opened a small crack, still being held firmly by a short, strong iron-link chain on the inside.

A plain, gray frizzy-haired lady of her mid-to-late fifties peeked around the opening.

"Yes?" was her only comment.

"Miss Devereaux?" answered Devon. "I'm Devon Stone and this other man here with me is Clovis James. I believe we have an appointment with you."

The woman laughed and closed the door.

The two men quickly glanced at each other. Devon shrugged his shoulders.

They could hear the chain being rattled and then the door opened wide. The plumpish woman stepped aside to let the two of them in and then she hurriedly closed and locked the door once again. The smell of photographic developing chemicals permeated the air.

"Miss Devereaux..." began Clovis James and the woman again laughed and held up her hands as if in surrender.

"I'll stop you right there, Mr. James," she said with a delightful Irish brogue. "As much as I'd like to be, I am *not* Drew Devereaux. I am her faithful, yet mousey assistant." She reached out her hand to shake those of the two men.

"I'm Francine Quinn. Drew will be out here in just a second or so. She's finishing up with a phone call. Phone's been ringing off the hook after that show opened a while back. Just, please, have a seat, will ya?"

The small entryway was like a tiny sitting area. As drab as the outside was, this room was clean and extremely contemporary. Stark white walls with several framed black and white photos, and sleek black leather Barcelona Chairs; sunken lights in the high ceiling lighted the area. Devon looked around, admiring one photo in particular. Both men turned around as they heard footsteps approaching from down the hallway leading to the front room.

Devon Stone had to keep his mouth from dropping open as Drew Devereaux entered the room. This is *not* what he was expecting at all.

Drew Devereaux stood perhaps 5'9", had long, wavy dirty-blonde hair gracing her shoulders, and sparking blue-green eyes. She was wearing tight khaki pants, a long-sleeved plaid flannel shirt with the cuffs rolled up to the elbows, and what looked like combat boots. She was ravishing.

Clovis James saw the look on Devon's face and inwardly laughed.

"Good afternoon, gentlemen," the woman said with a deep, husky voice as she reached out her hand.

Devon could feel his heart palpitating.

The two men introduced themselves, shaking her hand. She smiled at them both.

"We weren't sure if we were even in the right place," chuckled Devon Stone. "From the outside this storefront looks vacant and there's no signage advertising your studio."

Drew Devereaux laughed.

"I keep a lot of expensive equipment here, Mr. Stone. *Very* expensive. I don't want to advertise that fact by signage of any kind to invite the potential of burglary or having any windows letting the public view what might be inside. Photographic equipment is easily pawned and can be lucrative for the wrong kind of individuals."

"So then you must be aware of the reputation that this area has had in the past," quipped Clovis James. "Why, in Heaven's name, would you ever select *this* place?"

"Number one," answered the photographer with her hands on her hips, "the price was right. Plain and simple. Number two, Mr. James, if you've seen some of the places I've been over the years you'd realize that it takes more to frighten me than reputation."

I really like this woman, thought Devon Stone.

"Please call me Clovis."

"Just Devon here, Miss Devereaux."

"Very well then, and please call me DeeDee, that's what all my friends call me. And I have a feeling that we just might become friends," she said looking directly into Devon's eyes.

Clovis noticed that look and rolled his eyes.

"Please. Sit. What can I do for you? Francine explained a bit of what you mentioned on the phone, Mr. James, but I'm not sure I understand."

As if on cue, Francine re-entered the room carrying a tray with four cups of steaming tea. They all took one and Francine joined them as she plopped down on a chair next to Clovis.

After taking a careful sip of the hot tea, Clovis James retrieved from his jacket pocket a printed show catalogue from the exhibit at Whitechapel Art Gallery. He opened it to the page with the photograph in question and pointed to his late uncle.

"This man, running toward your camera, is my late Uncle Alistair Wallace."

"Oh, my! How interesting, Mr. James...I mean, Clovis. What a coincidence, right? You must have been surprised and delighted to see him in that print," she said with a broad, friendly smile.

"Well, not really," answered Clovis James. "Surprised? Yes. But delighted, no. Let me explain. See that other man? That little person seeming to follow my uncle?"

"Yes, I *do* remember at the time what a wonderful juxtaposition of the two men, tall and…well…shorter amongst the rubble, running from the danger of a bombing. I thought it made an fascinating composition."

"I know that that was twelve years ago," interjected Devon Stone, "but would you have snapped any other photos at that same time, either just before that one or immediately following? And if so, would you by any chance still have those negatives around?"

"Good Heavens," Drew Devereaux responded. "I may have. I can't quite remember if I did or not. There was a lot of confusion and bombs falling at the time. I had to snap my shutter quickly, as you can imagine. I'd have to go back into my files to answer your question, Devon. Why, may I ask?"

"I believe," spoke Clovis James, "that that little man," pointing to Darrin Rand in the photo, "murdered my uncle moments after you snapped that photograph."

Drew Devereaux suddenly sat back, put her hands up to her mouth, and gasped!

10

Drew Devereaux was thunderstruck.

"I remember now that as soon as I clicked the shutter a long, rumbling convoy of military vehicles came roaring down that rubble-strewn road, passing that area. I honestly can't remember if I saw those two men after the convoy ended."

"You probably *couldn't* have seen my uncle by that time. I feel certain that that little dwarf of a man, Darrin Rand, by name, pushed my uncle in front of those speeding vehicles. Uncle Alistair was hit, run over, and mortally injured. He survived in hospital long enough to tell my aunt, his wife, what that a little man had done. Devon and I know the history behind that bloody little freak and my uncle must have found out something that would prove fatal."

Drew Devereaux was almost in tears by this time and Francine Quinn was dabbing at her eyes with a hanky.

"And how, exactly, do *you* figure into this situation, Devon? Are you two men related, or what?"

"No, no," answered Devon. "We're long-time friends and his aunt and I were very close. Literally. We were neighbors. Without going into detail at the moment, let's just say that I had a past association with that man, Darrin Rand, which was far more than contentious. Clovis and I feel that the blackguard is long dead. We're just trying to resolve the issue of Alistair Wallace's untimely demise."

The foursome sat in silence for a few moments.

"I see," Drew Devereaux finally said with a sigh. "Well, then. It might take a bit of time, but I shall go through my files from that date to see what I might have that would confirm your story. Or at least bring some sort of closure. I can guarantee nothing in that regard, however. Sorry to say, gentlemen, that my time is at a premium at the moment. My current show at the Whitechapel is winding down and I'm preparing for two more. One in Paris and one in Manhattan."

Devon's eyes lit up.

"Speaking of Manhattan, DeDee, I am quite fond of that picture there," he said as he pointed to one of the hanging photos. "The Chrysler Building is my favorite structure in New York City."

DeeDee glanced at the photo and smiled.

"That photo was almost as dangerous as some of the wartime shots I've taken. I'm being somewhat facetious, of course."

The photograph in question was one of her perched atop one of the shiny, sleek, silvery metal eagle heads protruding from the Art Deco edifice.

"That *is* a wonderful piece of architecture, isn't it? And with those elegant Americanized versions of gargoyles. I was able to gain access to that perch and set up another camera with a timer to photograph myself as I photographed the city from the sixty-first floor. Believe it or not, my knees were trembling. I don't like heights!"

She stood up, signaling the end to the meeting.

"I'm so *dreadfully* sorry to hear that story about your poor uncle, Clovis. Give me your phone number and either I or Francine will get back to you should I happen to find anything."

Clovis wrote out his telephone number on the back of one of DeeDee's business cards and shook her hand.

Devon took DeeDee's hand and held it a bit longer than Clovis had. She looked at him with a warm smile.

"We came here for a specific reason and I'm *not* trying to be egotistical or anything, DeeDee. I really didn't expect it to, and it never came up in the conversation but have you, by any chance, read any of my books?"

She looked at him, cocked her head, and drew back a step or two.

"Books? You're an *author*? I should know you? Until you walked through that door I had no idea who you were!"

Clovis James laughed until tears were streaming down his cheeks.

At that exact moment, in a less dangerous part of town, Richard Fleming walked into The Poisoned Quill. His smile quickly faded when he saw that Amaryllis Cormier was not the one behind the counter but an older, dark haired woman. She was beautiful, in an exotic way, but not the person he needed to see. *Maybe she was around in the store, behind an aisle or two*, he thought.

"May I help you?" asked the friendly Lydia Hyui.

"Oh, maybe," Fleming answered as he slowly approached the woman, still looking around for Amy.

"At the recommendation by the young lady that works here, I bought a book a few days ago. I wanted to talk to her about it."

"Well, perhaps I can help you if you have any questions or concerns about it. That would have been Amy, the store manager. I'm Lydia Hyui, and I own this place. What was the book?"

"Oh? Oh! You're the one maybe I *really* need to speak with then," he said eagerly hoping for an even better outcome. "The book was *Wheels Within Wheels*."

Lydia smiled and nodded.

"By Devon Stone. Very good choice, young man. That's an excellent book. Why do you need to speak with Amy about it?"

"Yes, I'm enjoying the book very much. Those events and that bleak, sad time in our history were part of my teenage years. Amy is her name? Yes, I remember now and, as you said, it was Amy who told me that she...and *you*...actually know the author!"

"Devon Stone and I are good friends, young man. We see each other from time to time. Social gatherings, book signings...things like that."

"Do you suppose there is *any* chance...any remote chance that I might get to meet Mr. Stone? I've never met a real live author before and it would be a great thrill. Really and truly it would!"

Richard Fleming was laying it on really thick. Really and truly he was!

Lydia Hyui chuckled at the zesty appeal of this handsome young man. Knowing Amy the way she did, Lydia thought that Amy probably had swooned when the guy left the store.

"I just got back into town after visiting my brother in Hong Kong, so Amy had been pulling double duty for the past couple of weeks. I've given her the next week off to recover, so to speak. I'll speak to Devon and see what his schedule might be. Honestly, he's very accommodating and his ego is...well...it's a male ego, what can I say?"

They both laughed.

"Come back in next Saturday sometime and I'll have an answer by then. Who should I tell Amy came calling?"

"Joe. Tell her just plain Joe."

11

Once again Devon Stone sat at his favorite booth, in his favorite pub but this time it was with both Chester Davenport and Fiona Thayer.

As a rule, not many women went to pubs. It was thought that only prostitutes ventured into pubs. Refined ladies wouldn't be caught dead in one. Fiona Thayer didn't give a hoot about social dictates and decorum. She could drink with the best of them. Anytime and anyplace.

Directly behind Fiona, an old framed photograph hung on the wall. The photo was of a not particularly attractive woman, probably in her fifties, and probably at least twenty-five pounds overweight. A yellowing, handwritten note was placed off-kilter within the frame as well. *When I die, bury me under this pub. Then my husband can visit me seven times a week,* it read.

The photograph and note had been hanging there for over twenty years. No one could remember who the woman was.

"Your ego must have been shattered, dear boy," Fiona laughed.

"You stop laughing too, Chester, dammit!" said Devon. But he couldn't hold back the laughter himself. "She doesn't read fiction. But I told her I'd give her a couple of my books and she promised to read them. She's truly a fascinating creature, I must say."

Fiona sat back for a moment and studied Devon's face.

"There's a twinkle in your eye, dear boy, that I haven't seen in some time. If ever. Did she give your poor little heart a flutter, um?"

47

Devon Stone sat back in silence, contemplating his friend's observation.

"We just met for the first time mere hours ago, Fiona. Give me a break."

Chester Davenport chuckled. Fiona Thayer cocked her head and arched an eyebrow.

"Well. Maybe a little," Devon finally answered once again. "Actually, I felt there was a bit of a spark between us. It's not the gin speaking, but I can honestly say that I've never felt this way upon meeting someone for the first time. Aside from being a real beauty, she is just so bloody intriguing."

Fiona again sat back, inhaling deeply and giving Devon Stone that *I knew it* look.

"Ah, sweet serendipity," she sighed.

"Honestly," said Devon ignoring Fiona's last comment, "the ball is in Clovis's court at the moment. After seeing that blasted photograph he now desperately wants to find out more about his uncle's death, murder or accident. I'll just sit back and wait to see what happens."

"Oh, rubbish!" laughed Fiona. "Don't play the innocent dolt! Ring her up; ask her out for drinks…or dinner…or whatever. You promised her some of your books. Woo her with your murderous imagination. Nothing like a good grisly murder mystery to ignite one's libido!"

And they all laughed.

———◦⊰●⊱◦———

The following morning, shortly after 10 A.M., Devon Stone was ushered into his publisher's office. He glanced around and arched his eyebrows.

"Good morning, Devon," said a chipper and meticulously dressed Christian de Lindsay. "Thank you for coming in so promptly. Sorry for the short notice, but there is the possibility of a tour for you that just popped up."

"No problem, Christian. I was going to arrange a meeting with you anyway within the week. I want to go over the latest book that's sitting in my typewriter as we speak."

Again, Devon glanced around the office. He hadn't been in this office since he and Jeremy Fleck confronted his previous publisher about the murder of Fleck's father.

"I see that you've made a lot of changes in here since I was here last, haven't you?"

The previous publisher, the now deceased (by suicide) James Flynn, had a very masculine-looking décor. Dark, earth-toned colors, russet and burgundy leather furniture that looked as though it was stolen from an elegant men's club, and artwork depicting hunting scenes.

The chairs and the one small sofa in the office were now chintz. The artwork consisted of floral prints. There were two huge bouquets of fresh flowers on either end of the publisher's desk, practically obscuring his view of any visitors to his domain. A large framed photograph of a regal-looking woman sat on the corner of the desk, beneath a spray of flowers. She was smiling at the camera, and her neck was festooned with several strands of pearls.

"Is that your wife?" asked Devon Stone. "Very attractive," he lied.

Christian de Lindsay laughed, shaking her head.

"Oh my Heavens, no! That's my mother. A saint if ever there was one," he answered as he glanced lovingly at the photo. "She helped me redecorate this office."

"Oh," was all that Devon could say as he looked around the room askance.

"Actually," continued the publisher, "she's the second reason I asked you to come in today. We'll discuss the quick tour...well, the book signing...in a minute. But Mother just *loves* your books, Devon. Yes, believe it or not. And, just like our beloved Queen, Mother enjoys her spot of gin and Dubonnet every afternoon while she reads one of your books. When she found out that you're one of our authors she was *thrilled* to pieces. She wants to invite you to our place for dinner at your earliest convenience."

"*Our* place?"

"Oh, yes, Mother and I share her huge house in Kensington."

Devon Stone and Christian de Lindsay discussed a short, quick trip to Edinburgh, Scotland for some book signings. Three of the local bookstores had recently put in a request and Devon agreed being that he hadn't been to any of the stores in at least three or four years. He felt obliged. It was decided upon a date towards the end of March. Devon elected to *not* bring up his current book at this time and he stood to leave. The publisher stood as well.

"If your schedule permits, Devon, would it be possible for you to come to dinner...say...this coming Sunday evening?"

He couldn't think of a polite refusal that might sound legitimate so he accepted, inwardly regretting it.

"My schedule is open at the moment, Christian. Yes, I'd be delighted to come for dinner."

"Splendid! Splendid. Mother will be *so* thrilled. We'll be dressing for dinner. Shall we say eight, then? Oh, and please, Devon, bring a guest. I know you must have *plenty* of lady friends," he said with a wink. "It will be a lovely evening. I assume you enjoy gin on occasion as well?"

Devon Stone laughed.

On the ride down in the elevator he thought about the dinner invitation. He knew that Lydia Hyui was back from Hong Kong.

But this might be an excellent way to get to know Drew Devereaux better. After all, he had promised to give her a few of his books. Decisions, decisions.

Which one should I chose, he thought. *The lady or the tiger?*

12

Richard Fleming had just finished reading *Wheels Within Wheels* when his telephone rang. He knew it wasn't going to be a social call. Darrin Rand would probably be calling about that other little job that he had hinted about a few days ago. Fleming didn't want to discuss his thoughts about the potential Daniel Stein/Devon Stone connection. Whatever Stein had done to Rand in the past must have been horrific but, for the time being, it was of no concern. He was eager to see that sweet bird, Amy, from the bookstore again. First, for some potentially confirming information about the author. And second,…well…those thoughts were less than honorable. And *those* thoughts were giving him an erection.

———————⊃●⊂———————

Amaryllis Cormier was enjoying her weeklong vacation from The Poisoned Quill. She was almost finished being entertained by Miss Jane Marple in Agatha Christie's *A Pocket Full of Rye* but Winston kept poking her and wanted to go out for a walk. Although she and Winston had hiked the two miles over to Hampstead Heath on occasions, she lived in Primrose Hill with its own rolling hillside park and beautiful views. She rented a quaint little townhouse that was quite expensive but she considered herself worthy of it. Many of the shops and pubs within the area contributed to a somewhat bohemian flair, which she enjoyed. And it was a convenient short five-minute trip on the Underground down to the West End and the bookshop.

It was overcast and rain threatened but the two of them, canine and companion, saw a few others hiking around and playing in the park. She waved to a young couple with whom she had spoken in the past and Winston saw their dog, wanting to be set free to play. Amy unhooked his leash and he went bounding over to play with his canine friend, a big fluffy poodle. A few other folks strolled by and, unafraid or apprehensive, Winston ran over to greet them wagging his tail and almost begging to be petted.

"Oh, what a gorgeous beast you are," said the friendly lady as she ruffled Winston's ears.

"He's a real sweetheart," called Amy, "but I caution you not to bend over too far unless you want your face washed!"

The lady laughed and, obviously not concerned she knelt down face to face with Winston as, indeed, she was rewarded with a long wet tongue licking her cheeks.

Amy whistled and Winston came running back to her, sitting at her feet and looked up waiting for another command. She had brought one of his favorite toys to the park, a white tennis ball. She pulled it out of her pocket and threw it off into the clear area of the park.

"Get the ball!" she shouted, and off went Winston retrieving it within seconds and returning it. He dropped it at Amy's feet and looked up at her as if to say "Again, Mommy!"

Suddenly it started to rain and people scattered. Amy quickly hooked up the leash again on Winston's collar as they, too, started to run.

"Ohhh, come on, Winston. We have to hurry home. Sorry fella, but Mommy forgot her umbrella this morning."

"And leave your umbrella at home this time," Darrin Rand was telling Richard Fleming via the telephone. "I know that you don't like to get...wet, but this time I want you to make this as bloody as possible, if you know what I mean."

And Darrin Rand told Richard Fleming *exactly* what he meant.

"The filthy Irish twat went too far," sneered Darrin Rand. "Ya won't have any trouble spotting her. She hangs out around The Gallows, that rotten little pub down in SoHo. She's dyed her blasted hair as red as the Soviet flag...as well as her muff around her minge. Probably glows in the dark. Bloody cunt."

"I think I get the picture," said Fleming with a shrug.

The Gallows was one of the seedier pubs in the area and it almost seemed to be proud of its reputation. It was always doing a rousing business...even after closing hours. There were several rooms above the pub that smelled of liquor, cigarette smoke, and sex.

Shortly before 10 P.M. Richard Fleming sauntered down the street toward the pub, pretending to be a bit tipsy. The rain earlier in the day had passed and the streets looked clean and glistening under the old street lamps. There were more than a few "ladies" loitering about but, as Rand had told him, it would be easy to spot Maggie Flanagan, although no one really cared what her name was. Yes, her dyed red hair was ugly as sin itself, but she did have a somewhat cute face and a decent enough looking body.

This won't be as bad as I thought, Fleming thought.

He casually strolled close to her and smiled coyly.

"Are ya thirsty, lad?" she asked with a delicate Irish brogue.

"I might be," he answered. "But not for drink." And he winked at her. They started walking side by side.

"Do ya need some company, then?" she asked with eager anticipation.

He's a real stud, she thought. *Probably the best looking guy I've ever done.*

Richard Fleming stopped walking. Maggie stopped walking.

"Wannna come upstairs with me for a while?" she asked.

"Maybe for a while," he smiled and shrugged his shoulders. "I got rained on a little while ago and I think I might need to get outta these wet clothes."

"Oh, darlin', I can certainly help ya dry...off."

She gently took him by the hand and led him up some back stairs behind the pub to a dark, musty room. She flicked on a small lamp on a nightstand next to the bed and pointed to a chair close by.

"Why dontcha get yourself comfy, deary...if ya know what I mean."

He knew what she meant.

He first took off his jacket and laid it very close to the side of the bed on the floor.

As if to tease her, he slowly took off his shirt revealing his toned, smooth chest with the two tattoos.

She almost started salivating.

He unzipped his pants, dropping them slowly revealing strong, muscled legs covered with soft blond hair.

She, too, started shedding her clothes revealing firm, supple breasts. Richard Fleming smiled. She lay back in the bed, now fully naked.

Richard Fleming now had a raging erection that was clearly noticeable through his boxers. He slowly...very slowly slid his underwear off and onto the floor.

"Jaysus, Mary, and Joseph," gushed Maggie the whore. "You have enough cock there for *two* guys! I can't wait to bury my face in that nest you have there around that thing!"

Richard Fleming laughed.

"And I can't wait to taste that flaming red pussy you have there, sweet thing," answered the assassin.

He leaned over on top of her and eased his rigid erection into her soft wetness.

She let out a little squeal. Fleming didn't know if it was pleasure or surprise. Or if it was genuine or faked. But it didn't really make a difference. He started a slow rhythmic motion, sliding even deeper into her. His undulations quickened.

"Christ," she moaned. "You are a fucking machine! I might not have to fake it with *you*."

"Oh, you'll be screamin' in a minute, sweetheart, and you won't be fakin' it!"

And they both laughed.

Wait, thought the assassin, *just wait. You sure won't be faking in a minute.*

Fleming was nearing ejaculation but there was business first that need attention.

"I understand that you insulted and embarrassed a good friend of mine," he said, startling her and bringing her out of her pleasure for a moment.

"What do ya mean, love? Who?"

"The name's not important. But you'd know him if you saw him. He's a little guy. And I mean *little*."

He stopped his motion.

"Wait. Do ya mean that little freak? The dwarf guy?"

"Yeah. The one you called names and pointed out his… shortcomings…to everyone in the pub a few nights ago. He doesn't appreciate being made fun of."

"Yeah, he has a big old wrinkled, crinkled, crooked dick, did ya know that? Crooked as a dog's hind leg, it is. And balls like peanuts. Made me laugh 'til I peed myself. And what was that funny-looking hand all about, eh? Big fookin' deal," she said. "Get on with it, laddie. You're more than making up for it."

And Richard Fleming got on with it.

While starting to continue his gyrating motion he carefully reached down to his jacket on the floor and, with his right hand, retrieved his favored Fairbairn-Sykes fighting knife. He leaned into her, kissing her strongly and forcefully on the mouth to prevent her from screaming which he knew would be immediately coming.

With haste, he swiftly repositioned his hips withdrawing his rigid penis and forcefully, *very* forcefully thrust his double-edged dagger, up to the hilt, into her wet vagina.

Her eyes went wide with fear and pain as her body reacted with a violent jolt that knocked him off balance. He continued to push the blade further in and twisted it from side to side. He had to clamp his left hand over her mouth to conceal her frantic attempts at screaming and she bit down on it making him yelp. She tried desperately to get him off her as the pain was intensifying to a degree that was almost driving her insane. She thrashed around in terror, but he was too strong. With all the strength he could muster, he then sliced the blade upwards, ripping open her belly all the way to the navel. She suddenly became silent and limp. By this time his own chest and legs were covered in her blood.

He screamed out in sheer ecstasy as he ejaculated, pulse after pulse, all over her now listless body as he watched her bleed out and die before his eyes.

The next afternoon Darrin Rand laughed out loud with malicious glee as he read the blaring, bold headlines on all the London tabloids.

HAS JACK THE RIPPER RETURNED?

13

Richard Fleming awoke fully refreshed. Lying flat on his back, he stretched out his lean naked body under the covers and yawned. The night before he had had one of the most satisfying orgasm in a long time. The mere memory of it made him start to get hard again. He slowly rolled over onto his side. On his right buttock was a tattoo in script: *Kiss This!*

On his flat belly, between his navel and just above his dark blond pubic hair was another tattoo in bold capital letters: *SUCK THIS*, with a small arrow pointing downwards.

It was Saturday and he planned on going back to The Poisoned Quill to see Amy and perhaps find out if or when he might get to meet Devon Stone. Or was he really Daniel Stein?

Shortly after noontime Fleming threw his cigarette butt out into the gutter before entering the bookstore. When he stepped inside he was instantly deflated. He could see that the oriental-looking lady was there and not Amy. But, maybe she had the information that he needed. He slowly approached the counter and put on the biggest, fakest smile that he could muster.

Lydia Hyui glanced up.

"Well, then young man...you *did* come back," she said. She

turned her head toward the back of the store and called out. "Amy, your gentleman friend is here!"

Richard Fleming's smile changed to a genuine one.

Amaryllis Cormier came out of the storeroom with an armload of books. She approached the counter and laid them down.

"Hello, Joe," she said coyly. "I'm glad you came back."

Lydia Hyui smiled at this scene thinking that it could be the start of a budding romance.

"Did you finish reading *Wheels Within Wheels*, Joe?" Amy asked.

"Oh, yes!" he responded with faux enthusiasm. "So exciting. That Stone guy sure seems to know his stuff, doesn't he? Did he fight in the war, or something?" He was prodding.

"He can be somewhat allusive about his past. He's never elaborated on it, Joe," interjected Lydia Hyui, "but he…hmmm… how can I put this? He participated in the war in a clandestine way; let's just say that, so he writes from experience in that regard."

Richard Fleming feigned ignorance.

"Not sure I understood what you just said, lady, but he sounds like a real interesting fella."

"I think what she meant, Joe," said Amy giggling like a schoolgirl…and leaning in closely like she's about to reveal a big secret…"I really think he was a spy!" She whispered and then she laughed loudly.

Bingo! thought the assassin.

"Seriously? Really and truly a spy?" he said, laying it on really and truly thick.

"Well," answered Lydia Hyui, "I've only been told mere snippets. He doesn't like to talk too much about those times. He has never said as much, but I believe he escaped danger on several occasions.

He seems to work some of those events into his books. That's what makes them sounding so authentic."

Keep talkin', lady, thought Fleming. *Just. Keep. Talkin'.*

"I've got to run, Amy," Lydia said. "I just needed to get that paper work for my taxes. I know you two just might have a lot to talk about…about the book, I mean." and she winked at Amy.

Lydia Hyui gathered up a folder with papers in it, retrieved her coat from the back room and bid them a good afternoon.

The store wasn't as empty as Richard Fleming had hoped. By now there were several other customers glancing at books along the various aisles. He had to be subtle.

"Do you…" he pretended to be shy and embarrassed. "I mean… do you have a boyfriend or anything like that? Golly. Or are you *married?*"

Amy laughed so hard that all of the other customers turned to look.

The butter was beginning to melt.

"Good Heavens, you goof! No, to both of your questions."

"Well…perhaps…maybe…I don't want to be too pushy or anything, but would you want to have coffee…or supper sometime?"

Inwardly Amaryllis Cormier swooned.

"I think I'd like that, just plain Joe," she smiled.

"What time do you close up the store?"

"Today is Saturday, so we're open a bit later than during the week. We close at 8."

"I noticed that there's a nice little restaurant just down the street. How about tonight?"

Amy's heart skipped a beat. She smiled.

"Okay." was her simple reply.

"Oh, I forgot," said just plain Joe.

"I asked your boss last week if it was possible to meet that author guy. I've never met an author and I'd really and truly like that."

You can never use "really and truly" too many times, he thought.

"Hmmm...she must have forgotten about that. She never mentioned it to me," answered Amy. "But I run into him every once in a while when I'm out with my dog, so I'll be sure to ask him."

"Oh, so *you* know him, too?"

"Oh sure," she answered with a big smile. "Heck of a nice guy. I ran into him just not too long ago out there in the Hampstead Heath."

"He lives near there?" prodded the assassin.

"Well, not too far from there, anyway. Yeah, I think he lives in one of those nice row houses along Carlingford Road. I haven't been there, of course, but my boss tells me that it's very swanky."

"Oh, man...that's so cool," said Richard Fleming, feeling very proud of himself for his sneaky approach of getting results. "Hey, I don't want to bother you any more at work. I see that you have other customers. I'll see you later, then?"

"See you later, alligator!" she chirped.

What the fuck does that mean, he thought.

The Poisoned Quill was located within the popular theater district of London, the West End. On this Saturday evening, the area was swarming with patrons. The local restaurants were beginning to thin out and tables becoming available as the diners rushed through their meals to get to their 8:40 curtain times.

Richard Fleming arrived at the bookstore a bit early, so he poked his head in to see if Amy might be ready to close up for the night. Staying open until 8 on Saturday nights usually brought in customers of the theater-going crowd.

She was ringing up a few more sales. He ambled up to her and excused himself as he leaned past a customer and whispered into her ear.

"I'll head on down the street to Verrey's and get us a table. Take your time and I'll see you shortly."

He politely thanked the customer he had interrupted and headed out of the store.

"What a polite young man," said the hefty customer with three more books to be rung up. "And oh, *so* good looking! Your boyfriend?"

Amaryllis Cormier blushed and smiled.

"Not yet," she answered. "But I hope so."

Verrey's restaurant on Regent Street had been a popular place since 1825 and especially now with the West End theater-going crowd. With its high ceilings, low lighting, and excellent food it could be especially romantic depending upon the night and the patrons. Although there was never any music playing, it was still noisy at times with many conversations going on at once and the clattering of dinnerware.

Richard Fleming asked for a table that would be away from most of the foot traffic, both from the waiters and from the patrons. As he was shown to an appropriate table he noticed a tall, good-looking older gentleman carrying on a conversation with a couple of the exiting diners. It appeared that they all must know him. In fact, he was speaking with more than one little group of diners, with both men and women. Some shook his hand, slapped him on his back, and laughed. One man, however, seemed to be disgruntled with him for some reason and looked rather angry, gesturing wildly. That man's wife tried to disengage the two of them from the conversation.

Intriguing, thought Fleming.

The man in question stepped into a brighter light as he was bidding goodbye to the group and hurriedly made an exit.

Richard Fleming perked up as the man's face was illuminated better.

That can't be, he thought. *No. What are the bloody chances?*

The man certainly looked vaguely familiar.

Surely it can't be him.

The assassin called his waiter over to the table.

"Who is that guy that's leaving? The one that was talking with that group of people."

The waiter turned to look where Fleming was pointing.

"Are you an actor?" the elderly waiter asked as he turned back.

"No, sir, I'm not," he answered.

Yes, sir, I am, he thought. *In a manner of speaking.*

"Well then," said the waiter, "consider yourself lucky. He is both the most respected and most reviled theater critic in London. That was Clovis James, sir."

14

Richard Fleming was already on his second beer when, twenty minutes later, he saw Amy enter the restaurant. He stood, raising his hand to get her attention, and then remained standing as she approached the table. He pulled out her chair as she came toward him with a huge smile. He seated her and then sat back down.

"My," she gushed, "don't *you* look handsome? And a gentleman, too."

He was casually dressed in a black and white gaucho shirt (he had read that it was the current fashion trend for young men in America) with the top two buttons undone, and sleek, tight-fitting black trousers. He had slicked back his dark blond hair.

"I couldn't tell you that back at the store...not with my customers standing right there," she giggled coyly.

She was wearing a wide, full pale blue skirt with a broad belt around her waist, a white cotton blouse with Peter Pan collars and a small dark blue silk scarf tied around her neck.

"You look so handsome and I look so dumpy in my work clothes," she said with a shrug.

"Stop it, girl," Fleming said with a broad smile. "You could be wearing a gunny sack and you'd still look amazing!"

Amy blushed.

The grey-haired waiter, who looked as though he'd been serving ever since the restaurant first opened its doors, stood back awaiting their orders. He rolled his eyes and shook his head.

Someone's looking to end his evening entwined in sheets, he thought. *Lucky him!*

"Would you care for a glass of wine or a cocktail, young lady?" the waiter asked.

"Would you be shocked if I asked for a Bloody Mary?" she answered.

"I'm too old to be shocked by *anything*, miss," the waiter responded. "And would the gentleman care for another beer?"

"No," answered Richard Fleming with a nearly silent snicker, "I like the sound of the lady's drink. I'll have one of those as well."

"Very good, sir," said the waiter as he left the table.

"Actually," said Amy, trying not to sound embarrassed, "I thought that we'd be meeting just for a coffee or something. I didn't realize we'd be having dinner. I hope I brought enough money."

"What?" exclaimed Fleming leaning back quickly in his chair. "Don't be daft, girl. I'm calling this our first date. The grub's on me tonight. Eat hearty, lass…eat hearty."

They both laughed.

Their waiter brought them their drinks and returned a few seconds later with the menus.

They both toasted each other (Amy silently hoping for a long and close friendship, and Fleming hoping to get lucky before midnight), and glanced at their menus.

"You know what *I* do, Joe," Amy said as she was perusing the menu, wondering how expensive a meal she should politely order, "but what is it that *you* do for a living?"

Richard Fleming, remembering suddenly that he was just plain Joe, thought for a quick and reasonably honest-sounding reply.

"I'm in…finance," he replied with a gentle smile.

That sounds ambiguous enough, he thought.

"You mean, like stocks and bonds and stuff like that?"

"Yes," he laughed. "Stuff like that. Acquisitions and, you know, liquidations."

And he took a long slug of his Bloody Mary and watched her face.

The waiter returned and looked at them both.

"Have we decided, folks?" he asked.

They both nodded.

"And what would the young lady wish?"

"I'd love to try the Dover Sole Meuniere with the parsley potatoes."

"Very good, miss. Excellent choice. And you, sir?"

"How do they prepare your T-bone steaks here, my good man?"

The waiter didn't have to hesitate.

"Just prior to cooking the chef massages the steak with a little goose fat which will render a nice rich golden crust. It is one of our most popular dishes, sir."

"Sounds amazing. Then that's what I'll have. Medium rare, please, and with a crispy baked potato."

An hour went by and they conversed with basically small talk as they ate. Richard Fleming didn't want to appear *too* anxious to meet this Devon Stone guy. But, actually, he was.

Finally Amy glanced down at her watch.

"Good golly, Miss Molly! Look at the time," she exclaimed. "I need to scoot. My poor dog is probably wondering where his supper is...and has to go out!"

Christ, thought the assassin, *I forgot she said she has a dog.*

"Okay," he said, "I'll pay up and let's hail a cab."

"No, let's not bother with a taxi. I take the Tube to and from work. It's only a five minute ride and I live less than a block from the station."

Things were not panning out the way Fleming had intended.

"Okay," he acquiesced dejectedly, and he signaled the waiter for the check.

As they walked toward the Underground station he thought about reaching to take her hand.

"Come on up with me to my place," Amy said, "I know it's *so* cliché but I'll offer you some coffee to top off that fabulous dinner."

It *was* a fast ride, as Amy had said, and just a short walk to her apartment building.

As she unlocked her front door, Winston heard the familiar sound and came bounding out of the bedroom, tail wagging, where he had been sleeping up on her bed.

The dog took one look at Richard Fleming and stopped in his tracks. He even began to back up a few small steps.

"Winston!" Amy gasped in surprise and cocked her head. "What's the matter? That's not like you, fella. Where's that friendly, gotta-lick-your-face doggie?"

It was a slight, almost imperceptible move but Winston cautiously bared his teeth a little bit.

"I'm petrified of dogs," Richard Fleming lied. "Perhaps he can sense that. I forgot that you said you had a dog."

He saw the barely bared teeth. And then he elaborated upon his lie.

"I was savagely attacked when I was a kid by a pack of stray dogs. Took me years to get over it. I *thought* that I had gotten over it, but apparently not."

No, tonight would *not* end as he hoped for.

"Look, Amy...I had a perfectly wonderful evening with you and let's do this again sometime soon. Sorry, but I think it's best if I just slowly back outta here and go home."

Amy was disappointed but she understood.

"I'm so, *so* sorry, Joe. If I had known I could have kept him in a crate or something. Next time, though. And thank *you* for a superb dinner. Please let's have a repeat sometime soon. Hey, my treat next time!"

She wanted to give him a kiss on the cheek at least, but didn't know what Winston's reactions would be. She didn't want to frighten this handsome guy away forever.

"Please, Amy, don't forget to find out if I might be able to meet that Stone guy sometime and get him to sign my book. I really and truly would love to meet a real live author."

Again with the really and truly.

"I promise, Joe."

Richard Fleming walked back to the Underground station with a raging erection that would not be satisfied the way he had intended.

That fucking dog has got to go, he thought as he went down the stairs to the tracks below. *And soon.*

15

Early the next morning, *too* early for Richard Fleming's taste, the telephone ringing awakened him. He knew, of course, who it would be.

"Yeah, what?" was his normal way of answering.

There would be none of the normal amenities. No *"good morning"* or *"how are you?"*

"I went to that gallery you told me about. It was fucking crowded yesterday. Jesus, some fat broad almost stepped on me. She thought I was a little kid until she saw my face. Embarrassed the hell outta the bitch."

"Yeah, well?"

"Never saw that photograph before anywhere but, yeah, that was me alright. No mistaking *that*, was there? Handsome little guy, wasn't I? Of course I had much shorter hair back then. And no heavy beard."

"Were you two guys running away from a bombing…or was that building behind you in flames? Why were you running?"

Darrin Rand was silent.

The pause and following silence was unnerving. Richard Fleming heard Rand breathing on the other end of the line, which was a bit frightening.

"That other guy in the picture…Alistair Wallace…and I worked together at the time in MI5."

Why is this violent murderer being so hesitant to speak about this, thought Richard Fleming.

"I had no idea at the time that some dame was taking pictures all around the fucking place. I never even saw her. I was too busy doing something else."

"And so?" prodded Fleming.

"And so," continued Darrin Rand, "just a few seconds after that photograph was taken I killed Alistair Wallace."

Amaryllis Cormier fluttered her eyes open. The sun was throwing some welcome and warming light into her bedroom. Winston was curled up beside her on the bed. When he realized that Amy was awake he rolled over on his back expecting his usual morning belly-rub.

It was Sunday and the bookstore was closed. A lazy day. She thought about the wonderful start to her evening last night with Joe, and wondered about the sudden abrupt ending.

"Winston, Winston, Winston," she said as she ruffled the dog's ears and then began to give him his belly rub. "What was it last night, huh? I haven't seen you act like that with *anybody*. What did you see that I didn't?"

Dog lovers speak to their furry friends in complete sentences and expect an answer when questions are asked.

Amaryllis Cormier chuckled to herself when no reply came and continued the belly rub.

Huh, she thought to herself. *I don't even know his last name.*

Richard Fleming didn't know how to respond to Darrin Rand's confession of murder.

"I think I may have figured out who those two guys were that I saw standing in front of your photograph," he finally said following a few more moments of silence.

"Yeah? Who?"

"Well, one for sure and a big maybe for the other one. Do you ever go to the theater?"

"Don't ask such a stupid question, Fleming," laughed Darrin Rand. "I sure as hell don't go to no thee-ayters. I'd need a fucking booster seat, for Christ's sake."

Richard Fleming had to stifle a laugh but it was difficult because of the visual image that just shot through his mind.

"Okay then. One of the guys was a theater critic for one of the papers here in town. Clovis James."

"That's a big blank here, Fleming," said Rand. "That name means absolute zero to me."

"Oh, well. The other guy I know is Devon Stone. He's that author. I know, I know, we already covered this in our earlier conversation about this situation. *But!* I may have an answer for you soon, though. You thought the other guy could have been a Daniel Stein. I put two and two together. Stein and Stone. Get it yet?"

"What the fuck are ya talking about?"

Fleming couldn't believe Rand was being so dense.

"Look, I know for a fact that you speak German. Stein is German for stone."

More silence.

"If I find out that Stone *is* your guy Stein, do you want to me to take care of the situation in the usual way…if you catch my drift?"

"Absolutely *not*! I will take care of that bloody arsehole myself. I want to end his fucking life by my own hand!"

Hand was the operative word there.

"Are you sure?" asked Fleming. "When was the last time *you* actually killed anyone? Aren't you a bit out of practice? You *hire*

73

people to do things like that. I don't mean to be rude, for Christ's sake, but do you think you are capable enough?" he said as he nodded toward Rand's left hand.

"Watch your fucking mouth," snarled Darrin Rand shaking his right hand as a fist. "I'll figure it out, ya dumb shit!"

What are you gonna do, Fleming thought to himself, *bite him in the kneecap, you little pygmy?*

16

It was 7:55 P.M. Sunday evening as Devon Stone parked his car in front of the elegant detached house on Abbotsbury Road in Kensington belonging to his publisher...or his mother. Or both. His brand new, sleek sky-blue Armstrong Siddeley Sapphire 236, with its distinctive V-shaped radiator grille and a glistening silver Sphinx as a hood ornament, was his recent reward to himself for his last book outselling all of his others.

Dressed for dinner in his finest tuxedo, he turned his head and smiled at his beautiful companion. He got out of the car and went around to the passenger side to open the door and politely help her out.

Also dressed for dinner in a full-length, form-fitting emerald green dress, Drew Devereaux extended her hand and smiled at him.

A low brick wall with an unlocked black iron gate led to the walk up to the two-story house that was obviously a couple hundred years old. Huge old trees hung over the roof and outdoor lighting made for a striking, dramatic appearance.

Side by side, they silently strolled up to the front door.

Devon Stone was hesitant to take hold of her hand. But he wanted to.

Drew Devereaux was hesitant to have her escort take her arm. But she wanted him to.

Christian de Lindsay must have been watching out of the window because he opened the door before they even managed to ring the bell.

"Greetings!" he exclaimed excitedly, shaking Devon's hand and giving Devon's date a look-over. "This is so exciting. So glad that you could come."

He ushered them both into the elegant foyer.

Devon Stone made the polite introduction to his publisher and then raised his eyebrows as an elegantly attired older woman slowly came sashaying down the grand staircase, step by step, into the foyer. It was as if she were trying to make a grand entrance.

"And *this* is Mother", the publisher announced as if introducing the Queen.

Devon Stone extended his hand.

"Mrs. De Lindsay..." Devon began, and the woman held up her hand.

"No, no, no, dear boy. I'm Mrs. Landis now," and she laughed. "Christian's father, Claude de Lindsay, was my *first* husband. I've gone through three of them now. Each one up and dying on me. And each one leaving me richer than the last. Good thing you're not a bit older, Mr. Stone, or I'd have my hooks out for you! Not that I wouldn't favor a younger man, mind you."

Everyone laughed, although Christian looked somewhat embarrassed.

Good lord, a cheerful Black Widow, thought Devon.

Drew Devereaux decided it was time for her to speak up. Being reserved was *not* her best attribute.

"Good evening, Mrs. Landis," she said as she extended her hand. "It's so nice to be invited to such an elegant abode. I'm Drew..."

"Oh, my goodness gracious!" exclaimed the cheerful widow, clutching her pearls. "I know who *you* are! I saw your installation at Whitechapel just last week. I just may faint dead away. A world-famous author *and* a world-famous photographer under the same roof. *My* roof!"

Neither the author nor the photographer knew how to respond, so they merely smiled.

When Devon Stone had telephoned Drew Devereaux at her studio earlier in the week he wasn't sure what her response might be. He wanted to get to know her better, but was an invitation to a formal dinner the right way to start? It could be awkward. They chatted briefly on the phone and when he finally got around to the invitation she was silent for a moment.

"Normally I'm wearing trousers, for obvious reasons, Devon, and rarely wear skirts," she had said. "I have one formal dress and it's a few years old. Hasn't even been unwrapped yet after getting it back from the cleaners. And, for the life of me, I can't even remember for what occasion it was worn. I don't know where this might progress but, well,…okay. Yes, thank you for the invitation and I'll go with you."

They continued to chat for several more minutes and then she gave him her home address. When he went to pick her up he had brought three of his books for her. They chatted politely and a bit apprehensively on the drive to the publisher's house.

"Please just call me Maude," said the older woman, motioning them to follow her, "and please come on in to the parlor. Christian, darling, be a dear and get us our drinks, will you?"

Christian asked what his guests would like and quickly left to fulfill their requests.

Maude Landis ushered them into a spacious room, which Devon thought was a larger version of what her son's office now resembled. Chintz and floras. Pastoral pastels. He rolled his eyes and didn't fail to notice that Drew…DeeDee…did exactly the same.

A few minutes later Christian reentered the room carrying a tray with their drinks. Two parts Dubonnet and one part gin for his mother, Gimlets for both Drew Devereaux and himself, and a gin and tonic for Devon.

They toasted to each other's health and Drew inhaled deeply.

"My," she said, "something is smelling heavenly. One of you...or both of you must have prepared a sumptuous feast for this evening."

Christian de Lindsay nearly choked on his drink as he broke out laughing.

"Mother wandered into the kitchen quite by accident several years ago and got so frightened by all the appliances that she's never gone back in."

"Oh, hush, Christian," his mother kiddingly scolded. "But neither one of us can cook a lick. I was fortunate enough, years and years ago, to snatch and hire a wonderful cook from that old restaurant Danny's Steak House just as it was shuttering its doors."

Devon's heart skipped a beat.

Devon Stone, ne Daniel Stein, shared his father's name. It was Devon's parents who had owned Danny's Steak House. Sweet, innocent Devon Stone had lost his virginity at fifteen to the restaurant's sous chef, Vicky Jayne, who was seven years his senior. He had fictitiously worked that little tryst into his very first novel, *A Taste For Murder*.

"No," continued Maude Landis, "Vicky has been a godsend."

Oh, Christ, Devon thought. *This could be very awkward!*

Two more rounds of drinks, with much idle chatter and laughs, and then it was time for dinner. Devon Stone braced himself for a possible catastrophe. They were ushered into a large formal dining room with an equal amount of chintz and floral patterns on everything. This time Devon and DeeDee glanced at one another as he inconspicuously winked. She smiled.

After they were seated, Maude Landis rang a little crystal bell that was by her place setting on the table. The cook, looking to be in her late fifties, entered the room carrying a tray with prawn cocktails for the appetizers. Devon stared at her. Thirty-six years had changed them both. A lot.

She might have been a saucy sous chef at one time but now she was plump as a dumpling.

There was no obvious recognition by the cook and Devon Stone breathed a sigh of relief.

During the cocktail hour, the conversation had revolved around Devon Stone and his books with Maude Landis gushing over each and every one of them.

"I'm curious, Devon," the hostess had said, "about your thoughts as you write. Your imagination must be dark, I would think, to come up with those horrendous crimes and the *brutal* methods of murder. I assume it's not from first-hand knowledge. You certainly don't look like the murdering kind."

And then she giggled.

"Let's just say, Maude, that I do a lot of research."

And he smiled.

At the dinner table Maude now turned her attention to Drew Devereaux.

"Well, my dear, you certainly have captured two horrible conflicts with your vivid photography. First that horrible world war and then Korea. Brave. So brave of you for someone so young and beautiful. Any plans to just settle down now and do what *civilized* ladies do?"

Devon Stone almost did a double take.

Drew Devereaux was taken aback by the abruptness...and rudeness of that last statement.

At that precise moment Christian de Lindsay wanted to strangle his mother, saint that she was.

"That didn't come out the way I intended, dear. Sorry about that. I really meant are you going to concentrate on more peaceful endeavors?"

Drew Devereaux collected her thoughts and smiled politely. She took a sip of the Chambolle-Musigny, set it down and smiled once again.

"To be perfectly honest with you, Maude, *LIFE* magazine has been hounding me once again. As much as we all probably don't like to acknowledge it, the Viet Nam situation is heating up by the hour. I may be lacing up my combat boots within the next few weeks."

Devon's heart sank.

17

Three hours later, as Devon pulled his car away from the curb and onto the road, the ride back to Drew's home began as a silent one. A few minutes later a snicker came from the left side of the front seat. The passenger side. It grew into a heartier laugh.

"Mr. Stone," Drew continued to snicker, "I have to honestly say that this was the most bizarre first date that I've had within memory."

Devon was momentarily stunned.

"So...you're considering this evening a date?"

"What else would you like to call it? Yes, it may have been weird. A teensy bit uncomfortable at times, but I considered it a first date. I sincerely hope that it won't be the last."

They looked at each other and smiled.

I really, really like this fascinating woman, he thought to himself.

A late Sunday night in Kensington and there was very little other traffic on the streets.

Drew Devereaux broke the silence once again.

"I hope you won't be offended by this, but your publisher is certainly a strange duck, isn't he?"

"For someone who now runs a major publishing house, I'm surprised that he doesn't trip over his mother's apron strings as he walks through the halls," laughed Devon.

"Can't happen, Devon. His mother doesn't cook."

Drew Devereaux lived in a small apartment a few blocks away from her studio on Duval Street. His car came to a slow, rolling stop in front of her place.

"Don't turn off your engine, Devon," she said. "I'm not the kind of girl who does things like invite a first date in for…coffee, and stuff." And she snickered again. "Possibly not even on the second or third. I have trust issues. I might not be a virgin, but virtue is its own reward."

Devon Stone laughed.

"Thank you, Mrs. Socrates," he said as he got out of the car to help her out.

"I'm impressed, Devon. You know the origin of that quote."

"Of course," he shrugged. "I'm a writer and I know things. But then, the notorious Mae West took that quote a step further as only she could. Virtue has its own reward but it has no sale at the box office."

Drew Devereaux laughed and shook her head as she stepped out of the car.

"Good night, Devon. Thanks for these books. Now I'm eager to read them. Maybe I shall be quoting *you* someday soon."

Thirty minutes later as he pulled his car into his gated underground parking area it was too dark and he was too preoccupied with thoughts about Drew Devereaux to realize that he was being watched.

18

Another early morning telephone call.

Christ! What now? Richard Fleming thought.

"Yeah, what? I found out where that Stone guy lives, by the way."

"Forget about him for a while. I've waited a decade to end Stein's life. What's a few more days or weeks, eh? If Stone *is* really Stein and he's some local writer, he ain't gonna be going any place too soon, you know what I mean?"

"I do. So now what?"

"I got a call last night from one of my...hmmm...clients. He wants me to do something for him. He told me who, but I know this guy he wants taken care of. He's a big fat fuck and the way my client wants him eliminated won't work for my...stature, let's just say. Do you know where that Harewood House is...up in Leeds?"

"Holy shit! Yeah! I do."

"Well, that ain't it. This guy's house is just down the road from there. It's a big old place anyway, just not on any tourist attraction list. I know you got a car, don't ya?"

"Yeah, I do. Maybe I should take the train up there so my car won't be spotted or identified by anyone. I don't imagine that cars like my Maserati are all that common up in that area."

"So," said Darrin Rand with more than a hint of sarcasm in his tone. "You're gonna commit a bloody murder and then idly wait at the station there for the next train? That may or may not be on time?"

"Who's the guy and what are the instructions?" asked the irritated assassin. "I'll decide whether or not I take the bloody train. I'll get the bloody job done no matter what the conveyance might be."

Leeds is 314.9 kilometers or about 195 miles north of London. Perhaps a little more than fours hours driving time. Fleming knew that there were probably forty or so trains running between the two cities on a daily basis, covering the distance in a little over two hours. He knew this because the year before he finally caught (and dispatched) a cleverly evasive "assignment". They were struggling on the train, between two cars, as the coupling rattled and swayed and the tracks were zipping by practically beneath their feet. Richard Fleming, quite by accident and sheer coincidence, timed his action perfectly. He thrust the embezzling stockbroker off the speeding train at the exact time that another speeding train was approaching them on the other track going in the opposite direction. The thrown man's body impacted the train's engine head on. Various parts of the stockbroker still have not been found to this day.

Darrin Rand read off the victim's address and relayed, in great detail, the request regarding method of death.

"So we're taking requests now, are we? Hmm...interesting. Sounds fun to me. Three thousand pounds for this one," said Richard Fleming matter-of-factly.

"Done," replied Darrin Rand in a heartbeat.

Shite! I should have asked for more, the assassin thought.

Devon Stone was in a quandary. He was very fond of Lydia Hyui, who was now back home in London. And yet, the intriguing photographer who looks equally enticing in beautiful gowns or combat boots was stirring his emotions.

He lay back, soaking in his hot bath with a fresh cup of steaming coffee sitting on the tub's edge. Would it be appropriate to call DeeDee to thank her for the delightful, albeit weird evening last night?

His thoughts were abruptly interrupted by the telephone. He stepped from the tub, grabbing a towel and quickly dried off as he headed to answer it. He loosely wrapped the towel around his waist and with still partially dripping hands picked up the receiver.

"Good early morning, whoever you are," he answered flippantly.

"Good morning, Devon, Christian here," replied his publisher.

Bloody hell, thought Devon Stone, *what can I possibly say about last evening?*

"Well, and good morning to you, too, Christian. I was just about to call you," he lied.

"I want to apologize for Mother's ...ummm...performance last evening. She can be a bit much to take at times. Sometimes her tongue flaps before her brain can stop her. But she loved having you both there. I hope it didn't rattle you too much."

"Oh, don't be silly, Christian. No, no. We both had a perfectly... wonderful time. That Beef Wellington was fabulous. I make it myself at times and last night's was superb. My compliments to the cook."

"Funny you should mention her, Devon. I have no idea why, but she asked me to give you her warmest regards."

The towel dropped from Devon's waist.

Richard Fleming had decided to drive to Leeds after all and not take the train. Before leaving London he stopped at his favorite off-licence to purchase two bottles of Chateau Margaux, 1953 vintage. He already possessed the intended murder weapon, although he had never thought of using it for that requested purpose. He purchased a brand new one, a bit more fancy, because he knew that he wouldn't be bringing it back home with him. The mere thought of what he would be doing made his groin tingle.

No wonder Tiny Tim couldn't do it, thought Fleming, making reference to Darrin Rand.

He was planning on stopping in Leicester, the halfway point, for an overnight stay.

His selection was limited. He wanted someplace small and not too pretentious, although he was concerned that his expensive car might draw unwanted attention.

He drove around; somewhat off the beaten path, until he found an old B & B nestled among some tall oak and ash trees. It was old, indeed, but not musty. It was comfortable, but not ostentatious. It had a bar nearby and a car park in the back. That's all he needed to know.

———⮞●⮜———

Late afternoon and Devon Stone decided to stop in at The Poisoned Quill to say hello to Lydia Hyui and ask about her brother, Jian, in Hong Kong.

"Oh, golly," said the perky Amaryllis Cormier, "you missed her by ten minutes, Devon. She had several errands to run following her return home and asked me to close up today."

Devon was actually a bit relieved.

"But, hey, since you're here I have a request."

"And that would be, young lady?"

"I met a guy. A *really and truly* cute guy, too. And he wears the *nicest* cologne. He smells heavenly!"

Devon had to laugh at the way she was gushing.

"Good for you, Amy. And?"

"Well, he bought your book, *Wheels Within Wheels*. He saw me reading it in here and I told him how great it was. He never heard of you or read any of your books."

"I thank you for initiating a sale, Amy. That was so sweet."

"But, wait, Devon. When I told him that I actually know you, he was *thrilled*. He asked if he could possibly meet you some time and autograph his book. He acted like a little kid, he was so excited. It made me laugh."

"I'd be delighted to meet your...what is he now? What do they say in the States? Your sweetheart?"

"I wouldn't go quite that far just yet. We just had a sorta first date on Saturday. But I *do* have a crush on him."

"Crush? That sounds dangerous. Doesn't that hurt?"

Amy giggled, shook her head and gave him the squinty side-eye.

"You were teasing just there, weren't you, Devon?"

He winked and they both laughed.

"So you had a first date, then. How did it go?"

"It started out okay. We had a great dinner down the street at Verry's. But it ended kinda weird. We took the tubes back to my place but when he came in he took one look at Winston and froze. I thought he was going to pass out for a minute. And Winston acted strange, too. He didn't come running out toward us. He just stood there and stared."

"Winston? The friendliest canine on the planet?"

"I know. Joe said he was petrified of dogs because of an ugly experience when he was a kid. Said perhaps Winston could sense that."

"Perhaps. So his name is Joe. Joe what?"

Amy thought for a minute.

"You know, he never told me what his last name was. I don't know where he lives. And I don't have a telephone number, even if I wanted to contact him. He's just plain Joe."

"Ha!" laughed Devon Stone. "If he tells you his name is just plain Joe Smith back slowly out of the room and then run."

19

Richard Fleming sat at the bar sipping a Scotch on the rocks. He had been smiling and winking at the beautiful young barmaid every time she passed his seat. But flirting was all that he was going to do tonight. He knew that sometime tomorrow he would experience an explosive release.

His intended victim was Julius Rathbun, a corrupt judge who, more often than not, ruled in favor of the defendant should the plaintiff be non-Caucasian. And vice versa. Not only was Judge Rathbun a reputed Nazi-hater, he was also a Jew and an oenophile.

Richard Fleming was going to have fun with *this* guy!

The assassin awoke early, bathed and then dressed. He wanted to make a good first impression on his victim, putting the judge in a more comfortable mood when faced with a strange person coming to his front door. He slipped into his slim tan corduroy trousers, pulled on his off-white cable knit sweater, put on his Irish tweed sport jacket with leather patches on the elbows and would soon top it off with an Irish Tweed herringbone driving cap. He glanced at himself in the mirror and fancied himself a far more dashing member of the Peaky Blinders, a violent but sartorially splendid street gang that terrorized Birmingham around the turn of the century.

He then headed to the little dining area. There were only two other tables with occupants, both of them elderly couples. They nodded politely as Fleming took a seat at one table by the window. The host approached the new arrival with two pots, one in each hand.

"Good morning, young man, he said. "Tea or coffee, sir?"

"Coffee will be ideal, sir," answered Fleming. "I need something to keep me alert on my drive back to London this morning," he lied.

"Full breakfast, then?" asked the host.

"Definitely! I'm ravenous."

A few minutes later the master of the house wheeled out a small cart containing what was known as a "fry-up". Fried eggs, sausages, crisp strips of bacon, sliced tomatoes, mushrooms, a slice of black pudding, and hot buttered toast. He set the plates on Fleming's table.

"Anything else the gentleman might wish?" he asked with a friendly smile.

"Oh, no, my good man. This looks splendid. Looks like I picked just the right spot to spend my night. Thank you."

"Thank *you*, sir. Enjoy your meal, then, sir."

Despite the fact that Richard Fleming had no interest whatsoever in the facts regarding any of his targets backgrounds, Darrin Rand had filled him in with enough information to make the assassin's "visit" plausible.

The recently retired judge had left his career in the courtrooms of Leeds as a wealthy man. He owned a huge house on the outskirts of town. He had been widowed for over a decade. His children, grown and long gone, lived overseas following the war. His very last case prior to his retirement involved the person from whom the assassin would be paid. Needless to say, that person lost his case, which ended up costing him several thousands of pounds. In this particular case, the judge *had* made the correct calling but against the wrong person.

———⟫●⟪———

Devon Stone's morning cup of coffee had grown cold as he sat at his typewriter pounding away on his book that he promised his publisher would be finished within the week. His words were flowing, but his mind kept drifting to Drew Devereaux. A thought suddenly struck him because of that photographer, and he reached for his telephone.

"Good morning, Chester," he said when his next-door neighbor answered. "I need to pick your brain for a moment or two."

Chester Davenport glanced at his watch.

"Stone, it's too early," he answered with a chuckle. "My brain shan't arise to be picked for at least another hour."

They both laughed.

"Very well, then. What is it?" Chester asked.

"Clovis and I recently viewed an old photograph at an exhibition."

"I'm bored already, Stone. I may need to spike my coffee."

"Seriously, Chester. In this photo was someone we both knew... and worked with, for that matter, during the war. He turned out to be something other than we had thought."

"Go on, Stone. Now my curiosity *is* piqued."

"Eventually he and I had an altercation that did not end well. Not for him anyway."

"Are you referring to that... *little* man? And I mean that literally."

"I am, indeed. Darrin Rand. I haven't thought about him in years. I know where he ended up afterwards. Wretched man. I wonder if the blackguard is still among the living and perhaps tormenting the other lunatics and doctors there."

———⟫●⟪———

Richard Fleming timed the remainder of his drive to arrive at his destination late in the afternoon. He found the correct address and turned his car into the driveway.

It was a long, winding gravel driveway surrounded by towering old sycamores and common ash. It was lined by common hawthorns, which had been planted and cut to form a hedge. The further he drove the more he realized, with delight, that the old house was not visible from the street.

The house itself looked a couple centuries old, with a stone front and a steep-pitched slate tiled roof. He counted three turrets, one on either end and one in the middle. Smoke was curling out from one of the four chimneys. The day had turned chillier from the few days before. There was a wide, circular turnaround in front of the path leading up to the front door. The path was lined with rose bushes, their blooms now gone. He slowly rolled his Maserati to a stop and took a deep breath.

"It's show time, folks," he said softly to himself as he stepped from his car.

.

20

Richard Fleming carefully lifted the canvas and leather satchel from his car. It contained the two expensive bottles of wine and a small giftwrapped box. As he approached the steps up to the front porch he heard music coming from inside. He recognized the piece by Mahler.

Another Jew, he thought to himself as he searched for the doorbell to ring.

The front door was huge, almost eight feet high framed with a moulded concrete arched top containing a concrete crest motif in the center and smooth concrete panels down its sides. Dark wood, the door itself was stained almost black. In the middle was an oversized knocker in the shape of a lion's head. He rang the tiny button that he assumed was the doorbell. And stepped back, waiting.

No answer.

Perhaps the music is concealing the ring. He lifted the handle on the knocker and used some force. The music stopped playing.

The door opened with force and there stood the assassin's target.

He is a fat fuck, thought Fleming. *Just as Rand had said.*

Judge Julius Rathbun, bearded, age somewhere in the upper seventies, stood slightly over six feet, and couldn't possibly weigh any less than three hundred and fifty pounds. He was wearing a burgundy-colored velvet smoking jacket that was just barely tired around his expansive belly.

Richard Fleming immediately whipped off his hat as soon as the man opened the door, and gave a slight bow. It pays to be *extra* polite.

The man stared at him and then glanced around him to see the Maserati parked in the driveway.

"I know that this is highly unusual Mr. Rathbun...uhh, Judge...er...I mean, your honor. I mean, coming to your home unannounced," stammered Fleming appearing to act flustered. *Act* being the operative word.

The old man wrinkled his brow.

"I have a gift for you, sir, a small token and a thank you from my beloved uncle. The man you awarded the correct decision in your last case. Your very last case, that is."

"My word, I don't understand, son. Who *are* you?"

"Oh, sorry, sir. My name is Kevin Mooney. My uncle was ecstatic with that decision. He is too ill at the present time to come here himself, so he asked if I would deliver it to you."

The old judge huffed and then stepped aside as he opened the door wider.

"I still don't understand, but come in here out of the cold. I have a nice fire going and get yourself warm."

Richard Fleming stepped slowly in to the grand foyer, with well-polished dark hardwood floors and elegant Persian rugs. Faded tapestries hung from the high walls. He could smell the wonderful aroma of burning wood. The house itself smelled old.

Judge Rathbun ushered the younger man into the drawing room where the fireplace was ablaze. There was an old victrola with a record still spinning silently on the turntable, the needle having been lifted from the vinyl.

"So you say this is a gift because of that blasted trial? You don't look familiar. I don't remember seeing you there. Were you in that courtroom with the rest of your family?"

"No, sir, I was not. My business keeps me very active and I travel a lot. I believe that I may have been in Athens at the time of your trial."

This time Richard Fleming was actually telling the truth. But not for long.

Enough of the playing twenty questions, thought Fleming. *Time for action.*

He carefully lifted one of the bottles of wine from the satchel.

The old man's eyes widened.

Richard Fleming handed the bottle to him and the judge clutched it like a baby.

"And an exceptional vintage, at that! 1953. Oh, my, my, my. It must have been in your car for your trip here. It feels perfectly chilled. Would you care to join me in a glass before you return to... wherever it is that you'll return to?"

Fleming pulled the second bottle from the satchel. The old man gasped.

"Yet another? Oh, no, your uncle was *way* too gracious and generous. Please, lad, stay with me for a drink. I'm a lonely old guy."

The assassin gloated inwardly. This is working like a charm.

He reached into the satchel and pulled out the small giftwrapped package.

"Uncle sent this along with the wine. I have no idea what's in here," he lied.

The man untied the package and opened it up to reveal a long, shiny silver corkscrew with a hand carved wooden handle. Oak.

"Oh, now that's a real prize, young man. Must have set your uncle back a few shillings," and he chuckled.

Richard Fleming could start to feel the beginning of an erection.

"Why don't you uncork a bottle, lad, and I'll get us a couple of my finest crystal glasses. Only the best for *this* wine."

Fleming uncorked one of the bottles with ease and carefully removed the cork from the beautiful new device. He laid the corkscrew on the coffee table in front of the two chairs in which they'd be sitting shortly. There was also an antique chessboard with the pieces in place on the large table.

Rathbun reentered the room, glasses in hand.

Richard Fleming filled both glasses to their appropriate level as the judge held them out.

"Let me hold your glass for a moment, your honor," said Fleming, "and please put that music back on that I heard playing as I came to your door. Mahler is one of my favorites."

"Oh my word, you have excellent taste for such a young, and dare I say handsome man."

Fleming was quick. As the judge turned away to head to the victrola, the assassin put down his drink, withdrew a small packet from his pocket and poured the colorless, odorless, tasteless powder into the old man's glass. It quickly dissipated. Ketamine.

He handed the glass back to the judge as the music started to play. His erection was going to be difficult to conceal if he wasn't careful. They toasted to life in general and they both took a sip. The wine *was* incredible, Fleming had to admit.

"Please, sit," said the old man. "Savor the moment. Maybe you could stay just a while longer. As I said, I'm a lonely old man. Don't get much company these days."

He took another sip and then another. Fleming filled the man's glass again.

Judge Rathbun didn't know why, but things were beginning to get a bit blurry. His head was beginning to feel quite light.

"This wine, lad, is going right to my head. Are you feeling as wonderful as I am?"

"Oh, I think I will be in a few more minutes, sir. Do you have a bathroom close by? I suddenly feel an urge."

"Yes, I have several, but the closest is right down the hallway there. Third door on the left."

"Thank you, your honor, I shall be right back."

He found the bathroom and slowly closed the door. It was a full bathroom, not just a toilet. He glanced at himself in the full-length mirror and smiled. He started to disrobe. He kicked off his shoes. There was a hook on the inside back of the door, probably to hang towels. He hung his jacket on the hook. He pulled off his sweater revealing his bare chest. Carefully folding the sweater, he laid it on the counter. Unbuckled his belt and removed his trousers, then slid off his underwear and socks. He turned once again to stare at himself in the mirror. His penis was fully erect and he could feel a drop or two of slick, sticky pre-ejaculate as he rubbed his thumb over the head. He opened the door and padded naked down the hallway accompanied by Mahler's Fifth symphony.

Judge Rathbun was leaning back in his chair with his eyes closed. As he heard footsteps he fluttered his eyes open sleepily. The drug was taking its full effect. When he saw the naked young man, though, his eyes suddenly popped wide open and he bolted up out of his chair. He started to wobble a bit uneasily as he stood.

"What the bloody hell are you doing there?" yelled the startled man. "Has the wine made you go crazy all of a sudden? What the fuck, lad! How uncouth!"

Richard Fleming walked boldly right up to the judge and gave him a strong, forceful shove. The man tumbled over backwards, knocking his chair aside, and landed with a painful thud on the Persian carpet. The assassin suddenly leaped on top of the man, straddling his girth. Rathbun tried to push his attacker off but didn't want to touch the man's penis that was throbbing now practically in front of his face. He was shocked and horrified when he saw the SUCK THIS tattoo but then he suddenly recoiled in abject terror when he finally noticed the twin swastika tattoos on Fleming's chest.

For an elderly man, the judge had more strength than Fleming had expected. He tried to rise, but the old man was feeling his limbs rapidly growing weaker.

He couldn't believe this was really happening. Was he hallucinating?

"Liar!" he screamed. "You're a fucking liar! Get off me! Get out!"

The assassin received a slow, soft knee to his balls by the frantic judge, but he barely noticed.

Richard Fleming reached around to the table and grabbed the corkscrew.

He placed the sharp pointed tip on the judge's forehead just below the hairline and started to press down...and then he slowly began to turn it.

The judge screamed out in confusion, pain, and terror. He started to thrash but the drug was beginning to *really* take effect now and he felt himself growing weaker and more helpless. More hopeless. Time was stretching out, lengthening, as the old man slipped into a dizzying haze from which he would never recover. He hovered then, only briefly, in that liminal space between life and death.

Fleming continued to twist the corkscrew as it dug deeper and deeper into the old man's head. The skin is thin on the forehead, but the bone is hard. There are twenty-two bones in the human skull. The frontal bone is not the thickest, but it was far more difficult getting through a skull than a cork. The old man began to twitch in weird spasmatic reactions as the blade entered his brain. By now Fleming was being hit by Rathbun's squirting blood. The man gasped, even near death trying to fathom what was really happening to him. Blood ran down into his eyes…into his nose…and then throat as he tried in vain to speak. Nay, to scream.

Finally the hand carved handle of the corkscrew was flat against the man's forehead and could go no further. The man's eyes turned vacant and his corpulent body was now limp.

Richard Fleming sat back on his haunches and had the most powerful, long-lasting ejaculation that he had had in months, pulse after pulse spewing his semen across the now-dead man's face and torso.

His release was so overwhelming that he let out a long, loud satisfied moan when it finally ceased. He stood up, penis still dripping, looking down at the fat man lying at his feet.

"Hey, judge," he said. "The verdict is in. I think you've just been screwed!"

He casually walked back down the hall, the dead man's blood running down his legs and sprayed across his chest. He showered in the bathroom, toweled himself off and got dressed once again, placing the driving cap on his head at a jaunty angle. Checking himself once again in the mirror, he was pleased by what he saw. The assassin walked back up to the drawing room and picked up the unopened bottle of wine and placed it back into the canvas satchel. He picked the needle up off of the record that had still been playing. He had never had musical accompaniment to his assassinations before. He picked up the satchel with the wine. He started to leave but turned and walked over to the chess set that was on the coffee table. He brushed every piece off the board except for two. He moved one of the pieces. And then with a finger he flicked one of the pieces over.

"Checkmate," he said as he slowly meandered toward the front door.

21

Devon Stone was just polishing off the last drops in his bottle of Port after dinner when his telephone rang.

"Stone," said Chester Davenport after Devon had answered the ring. "I may have some disturbing news to impart."

"I don't like disturbing news, Chester. I hope that you and Fiona are well."

"Yes, yes…nothing like that at all. We're fine. It was beautiful a morning today so we decided on a little train ride. A trip to the country. Make a day out it and find a nice little restaurant for a luncheon. After my conversation with you yesterday we made a hasty decision. We rode up to Stafford and went to St. George's Hospital. Remember…oh, blast…you remember *everything*! Anyway, that's where that Rand fellow has been held since '46. Not the best of asylums, I grant you."

"The best place for *that* blackguard, though!" answered Devon.

"True. I'll give you that. We spoke to the doctors and psychiatrists who had been caring for the bastard. Caring is too gentle a word, but nonetheless. Wretched place! They reiterated what we already knew. The man's mind was so depraved, so demented that they held little hopes for his rehabilitation."

"Pity, but I have no sympathy for that demon whatsoever."

"They told me his one goal in life from the very first day of his being committed was to murder Daniel Stein, my friend. He kept repeating it over and over. Every single day."

"I shudder in fear," Devon Stone said sarcastically. "I hope he is either long dead or that he rots his life away forever in that place."

"Why they never contacted you I'll never understand," Chester responded. "I assume that perhaps they were unaware that *you* are Daniel Stein."

"And just *why* should they try to contact me?"

"To warn you, Stone. To warn you. Not before slashing two of the orderlies' throats, Darrin Rand escaped three years ago and has never been found.

PART TWO

ENDGAME

"What's done cannot be undone."

William Shakespeare - Macbeth

22

December 29, **1940** – London, England

"Bloody hell!" exclaimed an alarmed Alistair Wallace, red in the face and waving his arms around. "Have you gone daft? Or, even still, have you gone *rogue*? What could you have been thinking? This is beyond reprehensible!"

Darrin Rand, code name Country Mouse, was pacing back and forth in front of his senior co-member of MI5. They had been working side by side since the war began and formed a bond. Until now. He had to try to come up with a lie. And he had to think fast. He was caught red-handed and could spell danger with a capital D. Treason? Prison time? The firing squad?

The small room of the building they were in began to vibrate with the loud sounds of airplanes flying overhead. Then the sounds of explosions as bombs were being dropped. They looked at one another as they both realized simultaneously that an attack had begun once again. The Blitz continued. Something must have hit the building they were in and they could hear the sound of it collapsing.

"This isn't over, Rand," yelled Alistair Wallace as he began to race toward the door and out into the street.

"Get your lecherous, treasonous arse out there unless you want to die in here. But be warned, I *shall* report this and there *will* be repercussions. Now move!"

Darrin Rand began to run. His short legs couldn't move him as quickly as his taller partner but he was following close behind. When they got out into the street Rand saw a long convoy of armored vehicles approaching from their right. There was rubble all around, making their running a bit more treacherous.

Country Mouse didn't have to give it a second thought. There were bombs dropping, the building they had just vacated was in flames. There were other people in the streets running, shouting, with shock and confusion all around.

At the right moment, Darrin Rand lunged at his partner's back and shoved him out into the street directly in front of the second vehicle in the convoy. To some it actually looked as though Alistair Wallace had stumbled over some large pieces of rubble. He watched as the tires rode over the man's body. And then he made himself disappear into the panicky crowd.

23

Devon Stone and Chester Davenport were finishing up with their telephone conversation.

"Now that we know he's on the loose, and has been, you must remain vigilant, Devon," Chester said with a somber tone.

"That was three years ago," Devon replied. "The demon might be long dead by now for all we know. Even so, he probably doesn't even know that Daniel Stein and Devon Stone are one and the same."

***

"That's him!" exclaimed Darrin Rand while looking down at the photo on the back cover of the dust jacket for *Wheels Within Wheels*. "That's Daniel Stein. He hasn't changed…a little older, a little grey around the temples…but he looks the same. That bastard!"

The little man always looked angry. Always wound tighter than a spring about to break.

Rand smashed his fist into the photograph, as if punching the author in the face, and then he threw the book across the room.

"His *name* may have changed but my goal didn't," he said. "*Now* my number one priority is the murder of Devon Stone!"

***

It was kept from the press. Unbeknownst to the general populace because the authorities wanted it kept quiet, at least for the time being, Scotland Yard was perplexed by a series of seemingly random but strange, violent murders.

A bookmaker on Whitechapel Hill Street; a prostitute in an unsavory part of town; and a retired judge up in Leeds. Fingerprints on a telephone receiver at the bookmaker's office; fingerprints on the prostitute's bed post; and fingerprints on wine glasses and a chess piece at the judge's residence all matched one as yet unknown perpetrator. Obviously these acts of violence were connected. But how and why? Apparently a serial killer of sorts was on the loose but, to avoid possible panic or nervous concern, the information containing all the unusual details was kept within the confines of the police department. And INTERPOL.

24

Amaryllis Cormier smiled when she saw Richard Fleming enter The Poisoned Quill.

And he smiled right back at her.

It had been two weeks since that abruptly ended first date.

"I thought I'd never see you again, Joe," Amy said. "I was afraid that Winston might have frightened you away for good."

"Sorry about that, Amy. I was terribly embarrassed by the ordeal. I'm going to try to get over that fear. Maybe I can come back and bring a special treat for him to win him over as I try to regain some confidence."

"You're a real man of mystery, Joe. You don't show up for a couple weeks. I don't have any way of contacting you...and I don't ever know your last name, for Pete's sake."

Richard Fleming laughed.

"A man of mystery, eh? Ha! I've been called many things but that's never been one of them."

Then they *both* laughed. He spoke the truth.

"Yeah, well...business took me out of town, Amy. I travel a lot, so it's difficult to know where I might be from day to day. Oh, my last name? Richards. Joseph Richards. But to you I'm still just plain Joe, okay?"

Richard Fleming stepped aside as a customer approached the counter to have Amy ring up a sale.

Amy sensed that something was a bit different about Joe today. Maybe it was that strange night two weeks earlier, but he was edgier. Not as...well, not as sweet.

A few minutes later the customer left, smiling and nodding at Fleming when she walked past. He smiled back and gave her a wink.

That made her day, the handsome egotistical assassin thought to himself.

"So, Amy," he said as he approached the counter again. "Have you been in touch with that author guy...what's his name again? Stone something?"

"Devon Stone. Yes, I *have* had a chance to chat with him. Only briefly, though. He's very busy trying to finish his next book. His publisher is breathing down his neck. Obviously he doesn't give out his home address. He doesn't want every Tom, Dick, or Harry to come knocking on his door. I *do* know that he's going to the Grand National in a couple weeks. He always goes. So maybe if you'd like you can track him down there and have him sign your book. He always seems to run into a few fans who recognize him there he tells me."

"That's a possibility," said Fleming. He already knew where Devon Stone lived. "Hey, I'm not normally this forward but maybe sometime this week I can come up to your place again. I mean...you know...to go out for dinner up there somewhere or something... and, well, so I can maybe get friendlier with Winston?"

And a bit friendlier with you, too, he thought. *In all the best ways.*

Something's not quite right, thought Amy. *But I can't put my finger on it.*

"Well, okay. Maybe I'll prepare dinner for us so we won't have to go out. How about Saturday? Around eight?"

"Great! That would be swell." smiled Fleming. "I'll bring the wine. I have a great new bottle. Something I picked up while away on business. And I'll bring a special treat for Winston."

———>❖<———

Darrin Rand paced back and forth in front of Richard Fleming. The little man had just arrived at the assassin's apartment and practically burst through the front door.

"So?" he asked. "Stone...Stein...whatever...where and when?"

"He's going to the Grand National next week. Perhaps there's your chance."

"I'm sure as bloody hell not going to the fucking races. I'll be mistaken for a jockey, for Christ's sake!"

Richard Fleming stood back with his hands on his hips.

"Think about it for a minute. That could be to your advantage."

———>❖<———

Devon Stone shuddered when he answered the telephone to discover that it was Christian de Lindsay, his publisher.

"I know, I know, I know what you're going to ask, Christian," Devon said. "I'm typing as fast as I can. I'll get my first draft to you by week's end. Then your editors can have at it and edit to their heart's delight, my good man."

The publisher laughed.

"That's fine, Devon. Splendid. Don't forget your book signings in Edinburgh are fast approaching. Oh, and another thing. The reason I called, actually. Mother and I are going to the Grand National in a couple of weeks, Devon, would you care to join us?"

"Well, Christian, I always attend every year with a couple of very good friends, and I intend to ask Drew Devereaux to join us. Why not let's all go as a group and make a big party out of it?"

———⟫●⟪———

The Grand National is a steeplechase horse race that is held annually at the Aintree Racecourse in Merseyside, England. The course features much larger fences than those normally found on conventional National Hunt tracks. Many of the fences can be quite daunting and the event, which has been run since 1839, has been called the ultimate test of horse and rider.

25

Richard Fleming was prepared.

His plan was simple, albeit characteristic. He already knew where Devon Stone lived. He imparted enough information to Darrin Rand to satisfy *that* guy's bloodlust who was intent on revenge. On Saturday night he would enjoy some sumptuous meal accompanied by expensive wine. Then he'd kill his hostess's dog. Fuck Amy's brains out. And then kill her too. Leaving nothing behind except a load of semen. He would then be out of the picture for good.

But sometimes plans go awry.

"Of course, Devon, I'd be delighted to go to the Grand National with your group," said Drew Devereaux. "I normally go every year anyway, and this sounds like fun. But, I'm sorry to say; I'll have to leave for the airport the day after the races. I have an assignment from *LIFE* Magazine and I'm off to Viet Nam."

"That scares me," Devon Stone answered. "I worry about your safety, but then, I know what you've been through and survived."

"Don't worry, Devon, I honestly think that things are quieting down over there. The Geneva Accords appear to be holding. All foreign military personnel have to be out by the end of the year.

Sounds like the plans are on target and a peaceful place should be on the horizon before too long."

But sometimes plans go awry.

———⟫●⟪———

Devon hung up the telephone when their conversation ended and he turned his attention back to the typewriter. His thoughts, however, started drifting to Edinburgh where he would be doing his book signings a few days following the Grand National.

Edinburgh…and Darrin Rand.

26

December **1946** – Edinburgh, Scotland

The very first air attack over Britain took place over the Firth of Forth soon after the war had begun in 1939. Scotland was a major industrial British stronghold and a perfect target for the enemy. Edinburgh Castle soon became a military hospital. And that is where Devon Stone, ne Daniel Stein, last saw Darrin Rand.

The war had ended, but not for the little man who, at one time, had been a trusted member of MI5.

Darrin Rand was confined to his hospital bed. Heavily sedated and restrained, with his left hand (or what remained of it) bandaged up to his forearm. The right side of his face was bandaged from his hairline down to his chin. He flitted in and out of consciousness throughout the day and thrashed like a constricted animal when he was alert. He yelled and screamed constantly, frightening the nurses and orderlies who attended to him. They were relieved when the required doses of morphine would take affect, quieting him for a few more hours.

Six weeks after his arrival and subsequent treatment at the castle his eyes fluttered open one late afternoon. The sun was shining brightly through a window on the far side of his room and he saw a man standing beside his bed. The man was in total silhouette because of the blinding light from the window. Darrin Rand squinted, thinking perhaps he was hallucinating.

But he wasn't.

The man leaned forward and down towards Rand's face. Rand's heart rate increased rapidly as soon as he recognized the tall visitor.

"Stein!" he screamed, and thrashed violently, trying to get ahold of the man. "I am going to fucking *kill* you! I am going to slash you to pieces, as you did to me. If it's the last thing I ever do on this goddamn planet I am going to end your bloody life!"

"Not very likely to ever happen, Rand," responded Daniel Stein. "You should have been shot or hanged for what you did. Instead you're going to be committed to an insane asylum probably until the day you die. Your heinous offenses were indefensible. I just wanted to make sure you heard *me* say that."

Daniel Stein then turned, leaving the room with a raving Darrin Rand screaming until his voice turned hoarse.

⟶≫●≪⟵

Devon Stone sat back from his typewriter.

The first stop in his upcoming book signing event in Scotland was going to be at Blackwell's Bookshop in Old Town, practically in the shadow of Edinburgh Castle.

Rand escaped three years ago, he thought. *Could the blackguard still be alive out there somewhere?*

Devon Stone then chuckled to himself as he remembered the last time he had to take the short flight up to Edinburgh three years earlier.

He had just settled himself into his seat on the BEA aircraft, a

Vickers Viscount, and buckled himself in when he glanced across the aisle. An elderly woman, appearing to be in her early eighties, sat with a look of fear on her face. She was holding a little lace handkerchief in both hands that she kept twisting and untwisting nervously.

That hanky should be in threads by the time we land, he thought.

Devon smiled politely and gently leaned a cross the aisle. He didn't want to frighten her any more than she appeared to be.

"Does air travel make you nervous, ma'am?" he asked.

"I don't know yet," she answered with a distinct Scottish accent. "I've never flown before and we haven't left the ground. I thought I would faint dead away just by walking onto this contraption."

Devon Stone couldn't help it. He laughed out loud.

"Let me assure you, ma'am, that air travel is far safer than you driving your car."

"I've never done that either, young man! But my older sister is not well and can't come down to London to get me, so she insisted that I fly there. Not take the bus or train. But *fly*, she said! It will be fun, she said!"

Devon's compassion grew.

"Again, ma'am, this is a wonderful aircraft. You'll find it to be quite comfortable and spacious. The world's first scheduled turboprop flight was launched by BEA in 1953, possibly on this very plane."

The woman sat back in her seat and stared at Devon Stone.

"Do you work for the airlines or something, young man? How do you know that?"

Devon shrugged and smiled.

"I'm just a writer, ma'am. And I know things like that. One never knows when useless information will come in handy."

Ten minutes later the aircraft's engines began to rev up and the airplane started its race down the runway.

Devon glanced across the aisle to the woman. She was leaning way back in her seat, gripping the armrests and with her eyes squeezed tightly shut.

"Jesus, Mary, and Joseph," she said aloud. "Agnes damn well better have a full bottle of whiskey when I get to her fookin' house!"

Devon Stone was certain that somehow he would have to weave that short episode into one of his books sometime in the future.

27

Metaldehyde is an organic compound used as a pesticide against slugs and snails. Often sold in pellet form, it is also found as a liquid spray. The pesticide, at times, contains molasses with an aroma that attracts pets. It is extremely toxic to dogs and cats as there is no antidote or specific treatment for metaldehyde poisoning.

Richard Fleming knew this. He was very well-read, especially when it came to killing.

He was almost as adroit with poisons as he was with his Fairbairn-Sykes fighting knife...or his umbrella.

For his own safety, he pulled on a pair of rubber gloves. He had bought a box of small dog biscuits and he spread a few of them out onto today's newspaper. He paused briefly and then proceeded to spray the dog treats with the pesticide.

With the dog treats safely placed into a small paper sack and in his jacket pocket, Richard Fleming rang the bell to Amy's apartment.

But something was not right.

He heard voices coming from within the apartment and one of them was male.

Could she have invited Devon Stone to surprise me? Fleming thought. *Shite! That presents a dilemma now.*

Amaryllis Cormier opened the door and had a big, wide smile on her face.

The assassin didn't recognize the man standing several feet behind her. He knew, though, that it was definitely *not* Devon Stone. The man had to be at least six and a half feet tall; weighing somewhere above two hundred and fifty pounds…and it appeared to be all muscle.

"Joe," Amy squealed with delight, "Come on in. This is going to be a *wonderful* evening. My baby brother surprised me by dropping in on his way to Paris. He'll be with me for a few days. Oh, Joe," she said almost forgetting to introduce the two men. "Joe, this is Aster. Aster this is Joe."

The two men shook hands and Fleming winced. Aster's grip was like a vice.

Well, Fleming thought, *my fucking plans have definitely changed.*

"Nice to me ya, buddy," Aster Cormier said with a nod.

Richard Fleming glanced around, trying to act cautious and a bit nervous.

"Um…and, ah, where's your dog, Amy?" he asked.

Amy laughed and shook her head.

"You don't have to worry one little bit, you big scaredy cat," she giggled. "Winston is spending the night at a friend's house. I wanted to make sure you would be perfectly comfortable and not pee your pants every time he looked at you."

Fuck it, plans have changed even more, Fleming thought once again.

⟡

Devon Stone and Drew Devereaux were dining at The Ivy, one of Devon's favorite restaurants and one that had been in great popularity since it opened in 1917. As they were shown to their table, the beautiful photographer drew some admiring stares from a few of the gentlemen diners and some raised eyebrows from a few of the judgmental female diners. DeeDee was wearing wide-legged black satin trousers with a white V-necked silk blouse and a long sleeved bronze velvet open front-cropped, shawl neck Bolero cardigan.

Trousers worn by women were rarely seen nor widely accepted in fine dining establishments.

Devon Stone thought she looked ravishing.

———————————

Richard Fleming held out the bottle of wine that he had brought.

"Oh," said Amaryllis Cormier when she saw it. "That looks *so* expensive. And probably not appropriate. We might want to save this for the next time, Joe. When Aster arrived I decided to change the menu for tonight. I'm making one of our favorites. My Mom's very own recipe and I thought that it would be special to share with you. Meat loaf."

"With mashed potatoes and green beans," Aster added excitedly. "Can't beat *that* combination, now, can ya?"

The assassin simply smiled and nodded.

———————————

"I think that I shall try your Finnan Haddie this evening," answered Drew Devereaux following their waiters question as to their dining selections.

"Excellent choice, madam. And you, sir?"

"Being that my lovely dining companion is feeling aquatic," answered the author, "I'll have your delicious Lobster Thermador. I was going to have one of your incredible steaks, but I shall reserve that for the next time."

"Another excellent choice. By the way, Mr. Stone, it's nice to have you back again with us this evening."

"Thank you, Alfred. And it's certainly a pleasure having you again as our bringer of exceptional cuisine."

Alfred smiled, nodded and backed away.

Another waiter brought their drinks that had been ordered a few minutes earlier.

"Here's to you, my dear," Devon smiled as he raised his glass. "And also here's to our winnings, hopefully, at the Grand National next week."

His glass of gin and tonic clinked her glass of dry martini.

"I shall *also* add, here's to your safe travels to Viet Nam. That still rattles me a bit."

"I'll be back home before you know it, Devon. Although that news I read about today about that downed and missing B-47 over the Mediterranean rattled *me* a bit as well."

Devon Stone paused for a moment and simply stared at her.

"I didn't read about that incident, DeeDee, and thanks for now adding to my apprehension about your going."

"I'll be flying on one of those B-47s. I've been on them before and they're my least favorite aircraft. Last one I flew on was too sluggish for my taste on takeoff and *way* too fast on its landing. Daredevil pilot, I suppose. I may have stifled a scream."

Devon Stone laughed.

"I can't imagine you screaming. Stifled or otherwise. Your photographic endeavors scream unmitigated *bravery* to me, my dear."

It had been a pleasant but boring evening for Richard Fleming. The meal was simply okay, nothing special. The meat loaf reminded him of something called faschieter Braten that he had had while fulfilling an "assignment" in Austria a few years earlier and also served with mashed potatoes. The Austrian version was tastier.

But the boring small talk, mostly Amy and her brother talking about things back home in the States, suddenly changed when Amy mentioned Devon Stone.

"I don't know if you ever go to museums or galleries or anything like that, Joe, but Devon was telling me about a strange coincidence he observed recently."

"Oh, really?" the assassin responded, now with great interest. "What was that?"

"Yes, well, he and a friend were at an exhibition of war time photos and his friend recognized his uncle in one of those pictures. Strange, huh?"

"How odd. Yes, I suppose that *was* strange. What was the picture?"

Now Richard Fleming was getting somewhere.

"Seems like his uncle was photographed while running out of some building that was being bombed. And some small little midget kinda guy was running behind him. Devon's friend thinks that the midget murdered his uncle almost right after the photographer snapped that picture. How weird is that?"

So that's *how the theater critic factors into this scenario*, thought Fleming. *Darrin Rand might just have yet another target.*

Richard Fleming noticed that Amy's brother was nodding off, probably just as bored as he was.

"Amy, I'm so sorry but I think I'd better drift off into the night. It's getting late and I may have to leave the country again on Monday. Enjoyed your meal and, Aster, it was a pleasure meeting you. Hope I'll be seeing you again."

Fat chance, he thought as he reached to shake Aster Cormier's hand.

Amy was a bit taken aback by his sudden decision to leave. She felt that something was definitely amiss. Maybe she had been wrong and he was *not* the sweetheart for which she was hoping.

Richard Fleming reached in and gave Amy a small peck on the cheek and was out the door.

"That was strange," she muttered out loud.

"What? Who? What did I miss?" sputtered her brother who had quickly nodded off once again.

"Park your car Devon," smiled Drew Devereaux as his car rolled to a stop in front of her apartment building a few hours later. "Maybe I'll brew some coffee. Then again, maybe I won't. I'd like to get to know you a bit better."

"Well," said Devon Stone with a wide smile on his face, "To quote that infamous Mae West once again: He who hesitates is a damned fool."

Before too long they had gotten to know each other *much* better.

28

March 24, **1956** – The Day of The Grand National

Parking is limited at the Aintree Racecourse on Grand National Day and spots must be reserved in advance. Devon Stone had a reserved spot, as he does every year, but he had a better idea. Rather than forming a convoy, so to speak, with his friends, a two-hour train ride en masse is better than a long drive and it could be fun. The Aintree train station was conveniently located directly across from the racetrack. Trains were running every fifteen minutes on race days so that wouldn't be a problem. The problem was coordinating schedules and getting them all to the Euston railway station, and on the same train.

But somehow they did it.

Being that Chester Davenport was Devon's neighbor, the two men coordinated on packing a disposable picnic basket of sorts to be enjoyed on the train. It was forbidden to take food or drink into the racecourse. Devon had just received, via post, a large chunk of his favorite cheese, manur, made by his elderly friend in Serbia. So he packed that, along with other cheeses, apples, grapes, thinly sliced cold meats, and plenty of crackers and bread. Chester Davenport added one of his freshly baked specialties.

So the plan was set in motion.

Darrin Rand didn't have a plan. He knew that Daniel Stein, now known as Devon Stone, would attend the race. Along with seventy-five thousand others. He had gotten to Liverpool the night before and hoped that he might be able to locate, *somehow*, his target. He managed to get jockey attire…colorful silks and cap. His stature would ensure his disguise as being benign. Concealing a weapon could be another sticky situation, however.

———◦———

The Euston railway station in London was packed by the time everyone arrived, but Devon's group of friends managed to locate one another before boarding. Devon introduced Chester Davenport and Fiona Thayer to Drew Devereaux, then introduced Chester and Fiona to his publisher Christian de Lindsay and his mother Maude Landis. Clovis James, running a few minutes behind, joined the group and was also introduced.

Maude Landis seemed to glower at Clovis James when introduced. Devon Stone caught that look and wondered why.

They all boarded the last car on the train and managed to secure all their seats together.

Maude Landis continued to stare at Clovis James.

"So *you're* that despicable critic, are you?" huffed Maude Landis. "We have been at odds regarding several productions of late."

"Should I even be the least bit concerned, Mrs. Landis? Is my post at the newspaper in jeopardy?" huffed Clovis James in rebuttal.

Devon Stone rolled his eyes.

Christian de Lindsay wished he had left Mother at home.

Clovis James was known throughout the London theater crowd as an extremely tough-minded and sardonic critic, lavishing praise rarely.

"For example, Mr. James," Maude continued, barely taking

a breath. "You raved about the recent production of *Comedy of Errors*. I find that Shakespeare can be a bit stuffy at times and that production left me quite cold. Nothing to laugh at."

Clovis James wasn't sure where this conversation was going but he wasn't enjoying the journey. He shot a glance at Devon.

"And you positively hated *Plain and Fancy* which I found thoroughly enjoyable. A wonderful ode to a bit of Americana."

"Have you agreed with *any* of my critiques, Mrs. Landis?"

"As a matter of fact, yes, I did. *The Threepenny Opera* appalled me. It was dreadful, wasn't it? On that, we both agreed."

Christian de Lindsay was hoping that Mack the Knife might be somewhere around and do him a favor.

But he wasn't aware that someone real and even more lethal *would*, in deed, be around at their destination.

At this point, so early in the day, Devon was beginning to doubt the decision of bringing this group together. He never thought that there would be tensions right off the bat, especially with these two.

"Do I have to separate you two children?" Devon Stone laughed. "Behave. This is going to be a fun day." *Three dead husbands*, he thought. *She probably poisoned them all with her tongue.*

The train was a mere five minutes out of the station, but Chester Davenport decided that now was the time to ease some of those ruffled feathers. He opened the picnic basket he had been carrying. He removed a covered plate and extended it to Maude Landis.

"I thought we might enjoy a few of my special little creations on our way this morning. A bit early for a sweet treat, but these are sure to please. *Please* try one, Mrs. Landis."

Maude Landis, with eyes still on Clovis James, huffed, turned her head and lifted the cover. Her eyes grew wide and, with the other hand, she plucked a big, thick chocolate brownie off the plate.

She took a tiny, little nibble. Closed her eyes then took a sizable bite removing half of the rest of the brownie.

"Oh my heavens," she gushed. "These are the best brownies I have *ever* tasted, without question. They're wonnnnderful! I haven't ventured into our kitchen in years, but I'd *looove* to give our cook your recipe."

Devon and Chester Davenport shared a quick wink.

"Thank you, my dear Mrs. Landis," Chester said with a chuckle and a wicked little smirk. "But it's a family recipe...and it's a secret I can't impart."

And Maude's cook has a secret of her own, thought a smiling Devon Stone.

———⟫●⟪———

Darrin Rand made the erroneous assumption that Devon Stone would be driving to the racetrack today. He decided to walk around to the far end of the car park, wait and watch the entry gate. Richard Fleming had told him what kind of car Devon drives, and there weren't going to be many like it driving in today.

After getting a couple of rude comments and some questions about why was a jockey roaming around in the car park, Darrin Rand changed back into a more normal street attire. There had been a few rain showers earlier and he accidently stepped into a muddy puddle. He cursed because his beautiful new, calf-high boots were dirty. He might be a murderer, wound up always like a too-tight spring, but he was fastidious about his attire.

———⟫●⟪———

Throughout the train ride, Devon and his companions played musical chairs...or rather musical seats, so that everyone got to sit and chat with someone else. Fiona Thayer, very interested to hear more about her exploits sat side by side with Drew Devereaux chatting about Drew's photograph exhibition; Maude Landis began listening in, but remained silent.

"I can't imagine," said Fiona, "you just standing there with your camera, shooting film while gun shots were going off all around you. And all that bombing. Those horrible bombs! The gods must have been protecting you, my dear."

Maude couldn't resist.

"God *is* good, isn't he?" cooed Maude Landis. "Oh, yes. With all that horrible bombing going on during the war I prayed that my glorious rose garden be spared. And it was."

"He's very selective then, isn't he, my dear?" asked Fiona Thayer with just a touch of sarcasm.

"What do you mean?"

"I assume that people were praying to God all over the country for their lives to be spared during the bombing but to no avail, and yet he spared your roses."

Maude Landis didn't know how to respond to that.

Devon Stone had to turn away to avoid embarrassing himself with laughter.

Another hour, Devon thought as he glanced at his watch, *and there will be a live version of "Murder On The Orient Express"!*

The clickety-clack, clickety-clack, clickety-clack of the train tracks and the conversational buzz from the rest of the passengers was all that could be heard for several more minutes.

Towns and countryside zipped by as they all stared out of the windows.

Chester Davenport leaned over to Devon, whispering into his ear.

"I knew we should have put something stronger than tea into those bloody thermos bottles," he chuckled.

Devon pulled a small silver flask from the inside breast pocket of his overcoat and winked at Chester.

"Well played, Stone. Well played."

They both laughed.

They would soon discover that the other two men in their group were also carrying little silver flasks. For that matter, Drew Devereaux was, as well.

Devon Stone and Drew Devereaux were finally sitting side by side again. She leaned into his shoulder.

"Your friends Fiona and Chester fascinate me, Devon," she whispered. "I have a feeling, however, that you are...or *were* something other than an author at one time. Is there something you neglected to tell me that night when we got to know each other better?"

Devon Stone glanced out of the window at the passing countryside.

"Sometimes," he said as he turned to look her in the eye, "it might be the safest to leave the past in the past."

Although he had a strong suspicion that his past might soon be colliding with his present.

"And besides," he chuckled, "when I'm older and grayer I shall probably write an autobiography in the future and wouldn't want to spoil any of the surprises."

Devon Stone would, indeed, reveal all, but he would commit his publisher at that time to *not* publish the book until six months following his death. The section in the book dealing with the Soviet Night Witches would be most damning because of its legality or lack thereof.

Drew Devereaux smiled.

"You are an enigma, Devon Stone."

She leaned in even closer and whispered into his ear.

"And I think that I may have fallen in love with you."

By the time the train reached Aintree Train Station, the little picnic basket was practically empty…as well as a couple of the concealed little silver flasks.

29

Darrin Rand was still lurking at the far end of the car park. Every fifteen minutes a train would pull into the station across the street and dozens of noisy, laughing passengers would disembark. Rand never thought to scrutinize the throngs and, consequently, Devon Stone was amongst the group that nonchalantly streamed into the racetrack entryway.

Devon's group went laughing and chattering to their reserved West Tip Seats. With money on the line, as it soon would be, these seats provided the best views of the home straight as well as the final fences on the course. Attendees here would also have great views of the Parade Ring and the Winner's Enclosure. There would be five more races run before the Grand National but Devon's group was just interested in the main event.

They all compared their individual betting practices, having visited their local bookmakers prior to the racing day. Devon Stone was the only one to bet only to win. The others had elected to bet each-way, which meant that their selected horse must finish in the first four.

"How can I possibly lose?" asked Devon with a sly smirk. "I placed my bet on the Queen Mum's own horse. She'll be here today, of course, and her favorite jockey Dick Francis will be astride. As I said, how can I lose when her horse is named Devon Loch?"

Along with a wink, Drew Devereaux gave Devon a polite jab in the ribs as the rest of the entourage laughed.

The race would be broadcast live over the BBC radio station, but Aintree Racecourse maintained a long-standing refusal to allow the race to be broadcast live or delayed by any television company. That proved to be unfortunate considering the surprising and shocking outcome.

"So, Mr. Sure Thing," asked Clovis James with a haughty tone, "how do you expect to spend your vast winnings?"

"I've had my eye on an early Jackson Pollack, and plan to add it to my collection," answered Devon Stone without hesitation. "He's not done anything at all lately, I'm afraid."

"Ah, yes," snickered the sarcastic critic, "Jack the Dripper."

But sometimes plans go awry.

"Well, I for one," chimed in Maude Landis, "find the silks for the Queen's jockey garish. Purple and scarlet...oh, my, no. My money is on Pippykin. Don't you just love that name? Isn't it darling?"

One by one they called out their horse's names. Drew Devereaux had a sizable bet on Eagle Lodge. Both Chester Davenport and Christian de Lindsay had placed their money on Wild Wisdom, while Fiona Thayer had favored ESB.

"ESB?" asked Maude Landis with a chuckle. "What kind of name is that for a gorgeous horse?"

"I don't know," Fiona answered with a shrug. "I just like the sound of it. But this is all just for fun anyway, isn't it?"

Their excitement began to grow as the horses were led to the starting wire.

Darrin Rand was getting frustrated. The race was about to begin and he hadn't spotted Devon Stone, ne Daniel Stein, anywhere. *He must have come in by train,* he thought, *how else would I have missed him, the bloody bastard.*

———————⟫●⟪———————

The horses were off and running and the noise from the cheering crowd was deafening. The flashing colorful silks of the jockeys brightened the dreary grey of the overcast day. Englishmen were reserved, as a rule, but not at the racetrack! And especially not at the Grand National. No doubt the Queen Mother may have been nipping on some gin and Dubonnet…and shouting along with the crowd, albeit with a bit more reserve.

Devon and his friends were just as loud as everyone else and Drew Devereaux's camera could hardly be heard as it was clicking away at the sight.

The horses had to round the course twice before heading into the home stretch and the finish wire. The roar from the crowd grew louder now, everyone cheering on their favored mounts.

Devon Stone was in his glory. His selected horse, Devon Loch, had cleared the final fence and was in the leading position. He glanced over at a cheering Fiona Thayer, giving her a wink and a shrug of his shoulders. Devon Loch was leading ESB, Fiona's horse, by five lengths.

Suddenly and inexplicably Devon Loch half-jumped into the air and collapsed in a belly-flop onto the turf.

"What the bloody hell?" exclaimed a stunned Devon Stone.

The entire crowd was suddenly shocked into momentary eerie silence.

The fallen horse's jockey was able to get his mount back on his feet again but he was unable to complete the race.

Therefore ESB was the first horse to cross the finish line.

135

30

Richard Fleming was sitting in his apartment, scotch on the rocks in hand, listening to the race on his radio. He was hoping that the broadcast might be interrupted to report of a startling event at the racetrack. He was *really* hoping it would have been a report of a shocking murder, not a report of the leading horse having fallen before the finish.

"What the fuck?" was all he could say when the radio announcer simply, although excitedly, commented on the weird behavior of Devon Loch, the horse, and not on the murder of an attendee.

⟶━◆━⟵

The race over, Fiona Thayer glanced at a crestfallen Devon Stone.

"Don't worry, dear boy," she said with a chuckle and patting him on his shoulder, "I'll be glad to share some of my winnings with you so you can buy that ghastly painting."

Devon Stone scowled... and then laughed.

Fiona Thayer was the only one in their entire group who had winnings to proudly boast about. All of their other horses finished far out of the money.

⟶━◆━⟵

Darrin Rand cursed himself for being so stupid. How could he have expected to not only locate his target at this popular event, but to somehow dispatch him and get away with it in such a public setting. He felt rattled.

Then he cursed his own diminutive stature. After all, he wasn't especially inconspicuous.

His long-festering hatred for Daniel Stein had clouded his senses. He was being too impulsive without thinking things out logically. But he *was* determined.

Perhaps his target had not come to the race after all. Rand knew, now, where the man lived. But he would still continue to look here before heading back to London.

———————

Aintree Racecourse was slowly emptying out, with the spectators, some ebullient, others not so much, heading toward the car park or the train station.

Devon Stone walked arm in arm with Drew Devereaux. Chester Davenport walked arm in arm with a smiling Fiona Thayer. Clovis James and Christian de Lindsay walked side-by-side chatting about a recent book that neither had liked. Maude Landis slowly walked several paces behind the entourage, limping slightly and cursing her aching feet.

They had to wait for a couple of trains before they could finally board and find seats.

———————

The train had just barely begun to move when something caught Devon's eye. A man standing outside on the platform, looking both ways from right to left as if searching for someone.

Devon Stone stood up and as the train moved forward he walked back toward to end of the car, keeping the man on the platform in view. Suddenly, for some reason the man on the platform looked up into the moving train car.

For the first time in more than ten years, and only for a few fleeting seconds, Darrin Rand locked eyes with Daniel Stein.

Richard Fleming turned off the radio. Evidently nothing unusual except for the mysterious fall of a horse had happened at Aintree. Did Darrin Rand even make it to the track? He was packed and ready to head off to the airport. He would attend to Amy and her dog sometime when he returned from Athens. He just needed to get his thoughts in the right place.

Until his telephone rang.

"Shite!" he exclaimed out loud. He knew who that would be.

"Yeah, what?" was his normal answer.

"I fucked it up with Stein," Darrin Rand said with anger in his voice. "I missed him somehow. I certainly wasn't thinking right. He's still on my hit list but I need *you* to take care of that damn critic. He, too, now knows that I'm still alive. I don't care how you do it, just make it nasty!"

"That's all well and good. I have no problem there, but how are *you* gonna take care of Stein, Stone, whoever? You fucked it up once, so he'll be on the lookout. He's no dumb ass. And let's be perfectly honest, Rand, you can't just walk right up to him and…well, do whatever it is you want to do."

"He has a new lady friend. He's hooked up with that bloody photographer who started this whole new shit storm in my life. Perhaps I'll just use her as bait."

Richard Fleming hung up the phone and shook his head.

He's an idiot. Using the photographer as bait, he thought to himself. *So fucking cliché. And it won't work.*

———⟫●⟪———

A telex came through to Scotland Yard from INTERPOL headquarters in Lyon, France.

Fingerprints positively matching those of your recent homicides have been found at multiple crime scenes within the past three years: Austria, Denmark, Italy, and France. Brutal homicides. No eyewitnesses. Semen was found on victims at each. Elusive perpetrator unknown/unidentified at this point. Red Notice in effect.

31

It was nearing closing time at the Holly Bush but the patrons, many of whom were drunk as lords, weren't in any hurry to leave. The running of the Grand National earlier in the day had left everyone in a giddy mood, especially because of that odd occurrence.

Every time the door opened as someone was exiting, raucous drunken laughter and conversation spilled out into the chilly night air. One by one, or in twos and threes, it was mostly men who ambled in one direction or the other down the winding Holly Mount on the way to their respective homes, still laughing and prattling as they went.

In the shadows a disgruntled Darrin Rand was waiting. He managed to track his prey down but had arrived too late to catch him at home. He followed him to this little, out of the way pub. And so now he was hiding behind a clump of trees and a brick wall. His calf-high boots were covered in dried mud from lurking around at the racetrack earlier in the day. He slunk further down as two chatting and laughing men passed his hiding place. Neither one was the man for whom he was waiting. He looked back toward the pub to make certain no one else was out and about.

He was getting impatient.

A slight chilly misty rain had started to drizzle, making him even angrier. He was tired. He was hungry. He was cold. He was shivering. And he was frustrated.

Thoughts from the turbulent past mingled with those of the uncertain present.

Five minutes later the door to the pub opened once again and the man's intended target stepped out onto the narrow sidewalk.

"Blast!" Rand said to himself silently as he pushed back into the shrubbery. His target was not alone. The two men started walking toward him as they chatted and laughed as two good long-time friends would.

They casually passed.

You bastard, he thought, as he glared at his target that, now, was practically within reach.

He then quickly, cautiously, silently stepped out from the shadows and onto the sidewalk, retrieving a Model 34 Beretta from his jacket. He raised his right arm, aiming carefully. The darkness concealed his sinister smirk. He waited until the two men were not walking as closely as they had been upon leaving the Holly Bush. Once, a decade ago, he was marksman. Although his hand was shaking, he was certain of a kill.

"At long last and once and for all, goodbye Daniel Stein…and Devon Stone," he chuckled silently to himself as he pulled the trigger.

He fired. But the wrong man fell.

32

Following a few too many pints of Guinness, Chester Davenport had tripped on the uneven pavement, pushing Devon Stone off balance as well when he fell.

At the same time as the gunshot.

Both men instantly turned around to look behind them. It was dark, but they saw a small figure in the shadows scampering off into shrubs.

"Was that a *child*?" Chester Davenport asked incredulously. "Bloody hell!"

"Oh, no," answered Devon Stone shaking his head. "I'm afraid that was no child. We both know well and good who that was."

In his stumbling, bumbling overly anxious effort to kill his prey and then in a frenzy to get away, he had slipped on the wet, slick pavement and fallen, letting out a painful yelp. Darrin Rand had dropped his weapon.

And something else.

Being cautious as they approached, Devon bent down. In the weak light from an old street lamp overhead he could make out the gun lying on the pavement. A few inches away from it was a telltale sign.

"What is it? Is that a glove?" asked Chester when he saw it.

It was a dark brown leather glove, obviously for someone's left hand. There were straps and buckles around the elongated glove.

Apparently the wearer just now falling on the pavement had broken a couple of the straps.

"In a manner of speaking Chester, yes, that *is* a glove. But it's not empty."

———◦———

October **1946** – Somewhere along the Royal Mile – Edinburgh, Scotland

Daniel Stein was following up on several leads. He was not the only one trying to apprehend the maniacal little man. The elusive Country Mouse, Darrin Rand, had been pursued for months by his entire team without capture. He was wanted for murder, rape, and possibly treason since the war ended the previous year. Rumors were that he had fled the country for the United States, but the rumors were unfounded. The report that he had been spotted in Paris proved, also, to be a false alarm. Members of MI5 had recently tracked him to Edinburgh but then lost his trail. Although because of his unique stature he could easily be identified, he was also cagey enough to remain in the shadows and out of public attention as much as possible. He had been taught well how to be evasive and discrete.

At last, one late night outside of Greyfriars Bobby pub on the Royal Mile he was caught. But he didn't go down without a fight. Happenstance and perfect heroic timing proved successful for Daniel Stein. Reckless abandon led to Rand's downfall.

After a few too many pints of Guinness from another pub down the street, the inebriated and now careless Rand went on the prowl along the rugged cobblestone road leading up to the Edinburgh castle, causing a ruckus drawing attention to himself and to the young woman who resisted his lustful advances. Letting out a shriek, she was frightened not only by the sudden attack, but by his diminutive size. At first she had thought that a child had molested her. It had begun to rain and the pavement became slick. He lunged for her and they both slipped on the wet cobbles, falling into a tumbling heap. Screaming loudly, she fought by scratching his face and when she screamed again he drew a knife. He was about to slash her throat when he was pounced on from behind.

Daniel Stein had been enjoying a rare relaxing late night in the Greyfriars Bobby pub and was at the door about to leave when he heard the screams. Rushing outside to see what the screaming was about, he was stunned with disbelief. When he recognized Darrin Rand, he was elated.

Bloody hell, he thought, *what were the chances?*

He grabbed Rand from behind and threw him to the wet ground. Rand was back up on his feet in a flash and lunged toward Stein with the blade ready to slash. Stein, trained in martial arts, thwarted the attack by kicking outward striking the short man in the chest. The kick threw Darrin Rand backward, falling down onto the rough cobblestone pavement once again where he dropped his knife. When he reached for his weapon Daniel Stein stomped with all his force down onto Rand's left hand, smashing it with a sickening crunching sound, severing ligaments and tendons, effectively breaking the wrist and most of the bones in the now limp, dangling palm. He screamed not only in sheer agony but also in outright rage. He tried grabbing for the knife with his good right hand but Stein caught the hand in motion, dragging the blade down the right hand side of Rand's face from the hairline to his chin, opening a gash. He then bled profusely.

By this time a crowd had formed, constables had arrived and an ambulance had been called. Edinburgh Castle was just up the hill from this fracas and it was still being used as a hospital since the war.

It was quickly determined by the doctors at the hospital that Darrin Rand's left hand was damaged so severely that it could not be saved. It needed to be, and was, amputated at the wrist and a prosthetic hand, covered by a brown leather glove, was later created for the man.

Daniel Stein had immediately informed the attending authorities of Darrin Rand's history, requiring his restraints while in hospital and, upon his discharge, being committed to a sanatorium for the criminally insane.

⸻ ✦ ⸻

Noisy inebriated patrons continued to exit the Holly Bush, none, obviously, having heard the gunshot.

Devon Stone picked up the gun and thought about it for a moment before then bending over and picking up the gloved hand as well.

Chester Davenport came up beside him.

"It might be dark, Stone, but I can see those wheels of yours spinning. I know, now, who that blackguard was, but what exactly are you thinking?"

"A couple of things, frankly, Chester. And now we *both* know that the weasel is still among the living. Obviously Rand must have followed me here tonight. And he was at Aintree earlier this afternoon. He was definitely looking for me. But how the bloody hell did he know where I would be? At this point, only you, Clovis James and I know about Darrin Rand and what he did. And only our little group at the race this afternoon knew that I would be there."

"Surely, Stone, you don't suspect…"

"No, no, of course not, Chester. That never entered my mind. I have another thought, though. Now I…you and Clovis as well… need to stay vigilant until we get *him* before he gets one or all of us. It's late. We both need to get back home safely. We have his gun and, well, a prosthetic hand of sorts. My feeling is that he's quite deranged and not thinking clearly and not acting wisely. This attempt, as surprising as it was, could have been successful. We both could be lying dead on the street here. But he missed, panicked and fled. Despite what we all might see in the movies, in reality murderers are quite often inept and blundering. As vile and violent as he was in the past, I believe that Darrin Rand has simply reached that stage of incompetence."

"And now what?" asked Chester Davenport. "He knows where *you* are, but how do we find *him*?"

Devon Stone didn't hesitate for a moment.

"It's way past our bedtimes, old friend," answered Devon. "But I shall be up early in the morning. After I finish my first coffee of the day I shall pay a visit to the Poisoned Quill for a chat."

33

Devon Stone was hoping that Amaryllis Cormier would be at the bookstore. Not that he was avoiding Lydia Hyui, but he didn't want to have to decline any invitation for more than an idle chat. But he had the feeling that perhaps Lydia was, indeed, getting a bit friendlier with Jeremy Fleck in Hong Kong.

He smiled as he approached the front counter and Amy smiled in return.

"Devon!" she squealed. "I haven't seen you in a while. Keeping busy writing? Or playing?"

She snickered.

"What does *that* mean, young lady?"

"Your publisher...your new one, not the killer...that Christian something or other was in here last week checking things out. He told me about a dinner party."

"So?"

"Getting pretty chummy with that photographer lady, aren'tcha?" giggled Amy. "Do you two play that game too?"

"What do you mean? What game?" asked Devon.

"Well, it *would* seem appropriate. Some of the more...shall we say, adventurous, rambunctious horny teens back in the States play a party game when their parents aren't around. It's called Photography."

"Oh?"

"Yeah, they turn out all the lights to see what develops."

Devon Stone rolled his eyes.

"Don't be so impertinent," he said.

"Have you come up with a theme song for her yet?" Amy asked.

"Okay, I don't know where you're going with this, young lady. I don't understand. What's this about a theme song?"

Amy Cormier giggled.

"Oh, I do a stupid little thing. I started doing this the short time I was in college. I had a horrible professor in English Lit. She was a nasty old biddy. So every time I saw her I started humming to myself the theme music to the Wicked Witch of the West…you know, from *The Wizard of Oz* movie. So I started doing that with *other* people. Coming up with appropriate theme songs."

"Have you ever thought of therapy?"

And they both laughed.

"What about *me*, Amy? Come up with any theme music for me, dare I ask?"

"Oh, yes, Devon. Of course I have. Considering what you do for a living, coming up with all kinds of murders, *your* theme music is *Funeral March of a Marionette*, for sure."

"Ah, by Charles Gounod. I like it, Amy. Weird, but appropriate."

Again, they both laughed.

"And what about you and that Joe guy? Any pajama parties yet in *your* life?"

Amaryllis Cormier was quiet for a moment. And then she let out a big sigh.

"No, Devon. That man has me confused. He seemed to come on so strong at first and seemed like a big kid to me. I thought that was endearing. But something changed. I don't know if it was because of my loveable Winston…or my brother being there. I *thought* we had an enjoyable time at my place and then…nothing. I haven't seen or heard from him in weeks."

"That's actually why I'm here this morning, Amy. You claimed that he wanted to meet me ostensibly to get me to sign his book."

"Right. He seemed very eager to see you. I remember only too well. He really pushed me about it."

"Did you, by any chance, happen to mention where I lived?"

"No…well, sort of, I guess. Wait. I think I mentioned the street where you lived because I told him about running into you on occasion at Hampstead Heath."

"Hmm. Anything else? Perhaps like mentioning the Grand National?"

"Oh, yes. We talked about that the night he had dinner with my brother and me. That really weird, strange night. I felt certain that you'd be at the race because I knew one of the horses had a name you couldn't resist betting on. We all had a laugh about that. I think I may have mentioned you and that critic guy who was with you at that photographer's exhibition."

"I see. What do you *really* know of that young man, Amy? Apparently he's a man of mystery."

"Why are you asking these questions, Devon? Is something wrong? Do you know something about him that I don't?"

"Not sure yet about that. I won't go into details, Amy, perhaps I shall write a book about it someday. If I survive."

Amy gasped, putting her hands to her mouth.

"Tell me, Devon. Please. What's going on?"

"An attempt was made on my life last night. By someone from my past. By someone who shouldn't have known where I would be. Unless someone informed him."

"And you're thinking that the informant might have been Joe?"

"Yes, Amy, I am. I'd also be careful, young lady. Joe might not be exactly who you think he is. If that is even his name.

<hr />

151

One might expect an erudite, sophisticated man such as Clovis James to live in a posh home of some sort, and one would be correct. Divorced once and nearly married twice following that, the critic now resided alone in the elegant King's Cross Apartments, which date back to the 1860s. The building overlooks Regent's Canal, a nine-mile waterway that flows quietly from Paddington to the River Thames. His two-bedroom twelfth floor apartment included a private balcony that overlooked the canal and surrounding grounds far below. Convenient to be sure, as he was within a brisk ten- minute walk to his office at *The Guardian.*

Despite the fact that he rarely entertained or had visitors, his apartment was totally and elegantly furnished in beautiful classic art deco style and could easily have been a movie set from the cinemas of the 1920s and '30s. His framed theatrical posters and his prized collection of glasswork by Lalique would surely become collector's items in the decades ahead. Himself a fastidious housekeeper, his apartment was always neatly kept, finding everything in its place with ebony, mahogany and rosewood cabinets and tables by Émile-Jacques Ruhlmann, Louis Majorelle, and Charles Plumet being constantly polished to high gloss and with nary a spec of dust on any shelf. He would often relax by reading in his favorite burnt sienna leather club chair from the 1930s. It was a luxurious comfort that he enjoyed sharing with no one other than himself.

Late in the afternoon Richard Fleming had inconspicuously followed the critic from the newspaper offices to his apartment building. He was hesitant about following him into the building for fear of being identified or described by security when the critic's bloody body was found. Actually, he didn't even know if there would be any security in the building's lobby. He'd have to check that out. He waited for ten minutes. Cautiously he entered the building and was surprised to find nothing but a bank of elevators and stairwells opening into the expansive but dimly lit lobby. No security desk. In fact, no one around. The problem being, now, was what floor did the man live on? There was no directory. No mail boxes with names or floor numbers. *Fuck*, he thought, *now what?* But if he was patient enough to wait, perhaps Clovis James might venture out in the evening after dark. And, if he was cautious enough, the assassin just might be lucky enough to help the critic into that canal after having been sliced to shreds.

Clovis James poured himself a glass of Capelletti and sauntered out onto his balcony. It was becoming a pleasant early spring evening and he could see a few lovers strolling arm-in-arm along the banks of the canal as a narrowboat floated lazily along in the waterway. A man was playing with his dog on the grass by throwing sticks that the canine would eagerly retrieve and a couple of the benches along the canal had a person or two sitting conversing or reading. A waxing moon was slowly rising overhead and would be high in the eastern sky at the approaching sunset.

Finishing his aperitif, the critic was now hungry and, rather than prepare his evening meal at home, he felt that a casual stroll to one of the nearby restaurants would be in order. He rinsed out his glass, dried it, and put it back on its shelf. He then grabbed a light jacket and headed out the door and an awaiting meal somewhere.

He had left his apartment, thereby missing by five minutes a warning telephone call from Devon Stone.

34

Richard Fleming, his Fairbairn-Sykes knife recently sharpened to its finest effectiveness, was well concealed within his light jacket. Darrin Rand had told him to make the critic's death a nasty one. He was debating whether or not to simply slash the critic's throat and be done with it or to first gouge out the critic's eyes. After all, he was apparently a vicious critic so why not render him sightless first…and *then* slash his throat rendering him voiceless as well. Or maybe slice off a hand, like Darrin Rand's. The assassin could feel the beginning of an erection just thinking about the possibilities.

Drew Devereaux was probably half way on her journey to Viet Nam, so Devon Stone felt that she was out of harm's way, at least for the time being. Or, at least, here in England. He wasn't sure if Darrin Rand or that Joe somebody even knew about her personal connection to him at this point.

Darrin Rand paid his taxicab driver, giving a more than respectable tip, and telling him to disappear. He was standing now in front of Drew Devereaux's photo studio.

Clovis James was almost back to his apartment building following his dinner when he heard someone call his name from down through the trees and apparently on the pathway along the canal.

Who the bloody hell? Clovis thought.

He hesitated because he didn't recognize the voice. But who would know him? And why are they down there? Could it possibly be another tenant from his building?

"Mr. James," called the assassin, "please, I need your help. I'm stuck. I twisted my ankle and it might be broken. Please?"

It was dark down in that area. There were street lamps at intervals along the pathway but the voice was coming from the shadows.

Clovis James looked around. It was getting late and there were no other people around who could perhaps help. But was this a trap?

Against his better judgment he slowly made his way toward the unfamiliar voice. He saw a figure lying on the pathway, appearing to be rubbing his ankle. The light from a distant lamppost beyond the figure caused the man to be in silhouette.

Richard Fleming could feel his erection begin to grow. *This is going to be so easy,* he thought, *the man will be dead and in the canal within seconds.*

The critic took a deep breath and walked closer to the fallen individual.

As he got close to him, the figure leaped to his feet and drew a long knife from his jacket. The blade caught the glint from the distant light and Clovis James gasped, and then jumped back, almost tripping over his own feet. The man was still in silhouette and, despite the fact that he had called out his name, Clovis had no way of knowing who the attacker was.

The man lunged forward, aiming the blade straight to the critic's chest, waving it back and forth almost in a taunting manner.

But one thing that Richard Fleming hadn't counted on was the fact that, like Devon Stone, the critic was trained in the martial arts. Although that had been several years ago, the critic was out of condition, and he really hadn't been very good at it to begin with. At least he was able to maintain a formidable defense. It was almost a comical dance. But potentially deadly. The two men ducked and parried for several minutes, grunting and groaning, before Fleming was able to draw blood by slicing through the light jacket and across Clovis James's right forearm.

James, remembering some basic offensive moves, grabbed the assassin's arm, bending it backwards with a forceful thrust and twisting it, putting stress on the man's elbow. That forced him to drop his knife as he growled in fierce anger.

Suddenly a bright light flashed directly into the face of the assassin, temporarily blinding him. But rendering him visible to the critic.

"Hey, what's going on there?" called a voice in the dark. "What are you blokes doing down there?"

The voice came from a man steering an old narrowboat silently down the canal. He had heard the ruckus and flashed on a floodlight atop the bow of his boat.

Clovis James kicked the dazed and distracted assassin in the groin making him scream out in surprise. Or was it indignation? The critic was knocked off balance by the strength of his own kick and he toppled to the ground. By the force of Clovis James's kick, the assassin fell onto his back, landing with a painful thud. It angered him to the point of hysteria and he tried to retrieve his lost knife but he couldn't see it. He scrambled around on the ground, frantically looking for his weapon. A futile attempt.

"Help the man down there, son," called out the man as he brought his boat to a slow halt. "Help him to his feet."

A teenaged boy, first grabbing a club for a defensive weapon, hopped down off of the idling boat onto the ground and assisted a huffing and puffing Clovis James to his feet. He wasn't bleeding profusely, but his arm still ached.

Not expecting to be overpowered and outfought by Clovis James, and then set upon by the men from the boat, the assassin made a hasty retreat through the trees. He had *never* failed before in any of his "assignments" over the years. His ego was shattered, as was his libido. No erection. No ejaculation tonight. He ran screaming in angered rage into the darkness, disappearing into the shadows.

"Are you all right, sir?" asked the boy. "I think you're bleeding," he said as he glanced at Clovis James's arm.

"I'll survive, lad," answered the critic, looking at his bloody jacket. "Thank you both so much. Your timing was perfect. I have no idea who that blackguard was but you both surely saved my life. How can I ever repay you?"

"No need, sir," answered the man on the deck of the boat with a tip of his cap. "No need. I've oft times thought that the pathway here along the canal was not a safe one for blokes to be wandering long after dark. Demons in human form, you know what I mean? Be leery from now on. Come on, boy, we must go."

Clovis James again profusely thanked the man on the narrowboat and his young son. The boy climbed back up onto his father's boat that had already been restarted. The critic waved to them as the vessel then continued to glide off into the darkness of the canal ahead with just the soft sound of the quiet engine puttering away. A smattering of moonlight filtered through the trees and skittered across the gently rippling waters. He watched them go and breathed a sigh of relief. His heart rate had finally come back down to normal.

He removed a handkerchief from his pocket and carefully picked up the fallen knife by the tip of the blade.

After attending to his wound, superficial but still painful, Clovis James called Scotland Yard to report the incident. And then he called Devon Stone.

———◦———

"Interesting and frighteningly intriguing coincidence, my friend," Devon Stone said after being told about the attack.

"How so?" answered Clovis James.

"Francine, Drew Devereaux's assistant, called me less that fifteen minutes ago. She remembered the story about your uncle that we both had told that day back in the studio. And guess what?"

"Sorry, Stone, I'm not in the mood for bloody guessing games tonight. What the hell is it?"

"Fortunately Drew is probably in Viet Nam by now, but someone came knocking on the studio door earlier this evening. A small man looking for the photographer."

"And by *small* man you mean…?"

"Yes, exactly. Needless to say, Francine never unlatched the chains on the door and told Rand that Drew was out of the country on assignment. And now I am of the opinion that your attacker and that *small* man are connected. But how and why?"

———◦———

After spending an exhausting hour with a Detective Sergeant of Scotland Yard the night before, Clovis James was awaked early the next morning by a telephone call from that same man.

"Good morning, Mr. James, Detective Sergeant Whitehouse here. I trust that I have not disturbed you in any way despite the hour," said the officer.

"Not at all," Clovis lied as he rolled over in bed trying to wake up. "But why such an early call? We met only mere hours ago."

"Oh, this is very exciting, sir. Very exciting, indeed! I thought that our investigation last evening was just about a random but violent mugging. But, oh, no! Your incident last night may be the one to break the case of a long, as-yet unsolved string of violent murders throughout Europe."

Clovis James bolted upright in his bed.

"Excuse me? *What* other murders?"

"I shan't go into details here, Mr. James, but can you give a good enough description of your assailant to have a portrait drawn?"

"I have a great eye for detail, my good man. Of course, I can. I can even describe the man's cologne that he was wearing. I wear it myself. That new Chanel Pour Monsieur. Again I ask, why?"

The officer chuckled silently to himself thinking about the expensive cologne. *A fop he is, no doubt,* he thought.

"The fingerprints we got off that knife match perfectly the ones that have been circulating throughout INTERPOL for that past few years. You are a very lucky man this morning, Mr. James. Apparently your attacker is a very sadistic and demented sex-crazed assassin."

At that exact same moment other men from Scotland Yard were sorting through the smoldering, partially burned ruins of a photography studio on Duval Street. The fire brigade had been able to squelch the blaze before it had been a total disaster but they had found an unsettling sight. The body of a female, burned beyond recognition, with a bullet hole in the center of her forehead.

35

Richard Fleming was beyond angry. *Way* beyond. Not only had he failed in his attempt to kill the drama critic, but also he lost his beloved knife. The weapon had been so effective in multiple "assignments" throughout Europe. He was hoping that the knife would have remained hidden among the bushes and weeds along that canal. Perhaps he *might* go back to look for it. Perhaps someone *might* find it and realize what a beautiful piece of weaponry it was and keep it for themselves. Or perhaps, he *really* feared, that it could be used as evidence in an attempted murder.

He had been extremely careful in all the previous murders, heinous as they were, to leave few clues, if any, as to the perpetrator. He was an unknown assailant.

But now he was mistaken. Only he didn't know it.

Darrin Rand was both angry with himself and proud that he had eliminated at least one person who could identify him. He had failed in his first attempt to kill Daniel Stein. When he lost balance and fell on that dark, bumpy pavement outside the pub his prosthetic hand was dislodged by broken straps and landed somewhere on the ground. He couldn't find it in the dark and left hastily without it. *And* he had dropped his gun. *Clumsy asshole*, he thought to himself. He had another prosthetic hand...and he had another gun. Several.

Richard Fleming's telephone rang and he hesitated answering it. He, of course, knew who it would be and he hated to admit a failure.

"Yeah, what, Rand?" he answered after several rings.

"I eliminated the photographer," Darrin Rand said matter-of-factly. "It wasn't my intent but I had to do it. I had no choice."

"Why? What happened?"

"I went to her studio and the bloody place has chains on the door. She opened it when I knocked, peeked out through the chains, and had the nerve to lie to me. When I asked to come in and talk to her she had the gall to tell me, quote-unquote, that the photographer was overseas on assignment and just go away. Bull shit, I thought. She then slammed the door shut."

"That was it?"

"Hell, no! I had no doubt that she was a liar and didn't want to do business with a freak my size. I get that all the time. Pissed me off. I figured there was a back door someplace. So I found it and busted in. The fucking photographer was in the darkroom. Scared the shit outta the old lady and she threw a tray of chemicals at me. I had no choice. I shot her in the head and set fire to the place."

"Did you just call her an old lady?"

"Yeah, a frizzy-haired old bitch, she was."

"She wasn't," answered the assassin.

"What do you mean by that?"

"Drew Devereaux, the photographer you *thought* you had just killed, is neither old nor frizzy-haired."

There was silence on the line.

"Sorry to tell you, Rand, but you killed the wrong person. You fucked up."

A long silence once again on the line.

Neither man wanted to let the other know that their targets had been missed. Daniel Stein and Drew Devereaux for the one, and Clovis James for the other.

But now forgetting the drama critic for a while, Richard Fleming thought about another target he should set his sights on before things get too dicey. Before someone starts talking. Two targets, actually.

A girl and her dog.

Richard Fleming went shopping. First stop, the butcher shop. He purchased a petite filet mignon. Second stop, the off-license. He purchased another bottle of that expensive wine…and another new corkscrew.

36

Devon Stone was in a quandary. He was due to head to Edinburgh for his book signing events the next day. But considering the recent attempted murders on both himself and Clovis James he pondered cancelling. *Not* a good thing to do at this stage. It would greatly anger the bookstores in Scotland and his awaiting fans, and rattle the nerves of Christian de Lindsay, his publisher. His publisher was a nervous Nelly as it was, thought Stone. After all, his publishing house was picking up the tab for the trip.

What the hell? I'll go, he thought to himself after a few moments of back and forth, pro and con deliberation.

It would be five days away from home, the first and last day being mostly travel. He had already purchased his tickets to and from Edinburgh and he was looking forward to a relaxing seven and a half hour ride on the Flying Scotsman. The historic steam engine with its long, heavy passenger cars behind would take a spectacular scenic route up the East Coast mainline. It was the first locomotive ever to achieve the speed of one hundred miles per hour.

The hours on board the train would offer him plenty of uninterrupted time to continue writing his next book. The manuscript for *I Dream Of Death* about the clairvoyant murderess was with his editors, and he leaped right into beginning another one. His typewriter would be part of his overnight luggage.

He was also looking forward to staying in The Witchery, a

four hundred year old hotel suspected of being haunted. It was conveniently located just a brisk eight minute walk from the train station, and taking even less time to walk up to Edinburgh Castle. All of the bookshops on his itinerary were also within the same vicinity.

Although he had never done so, nor ever had a reason, Devon Stone decided to travel with his new pistol, the .38 caliber Colt Cobra, which he had purchased a few months earlier.

Unless he would be followed from the moment he left his house, only Clovis James, Chester Davenport, and Christian de Lindsay knew where he would be and how he would be traveling so he felt somewhat optimistic about his safety.

Amaryllis Cormier had been home from work less than ten minutes when her front doorbell rang. She wasn't expecting anyone. Her last conversation with Devon Stone had made her apprehensive. She was tired and just wanted some time to unwind, perhaps with a glass of wine before she prepared dinner for herself. She hadn't even had time to take Winston out for his walk.

She looked through the peephole in her door and reacted with a jolt and stepping back.

Oh, shit, she thought. *What do I do now?*

Standing out in the hallway was her handsome just plain Joe. She couldn't see all that much through the round peephole in her door, but it looked like he may have a bunch of flowers. He was smiling sweetly.

She took a deep breath and opened the door.

37

"Joe, oh, my goodness what a surprise!" Amy said trying to sound friendly, yet concealing an inward dread.

Then she took a more straightforward approach, folding her arms across her chest.

"Where the *hell* have you been? I was just about to give up on you," she lied.

Richard Fleming took a cautious step into the room as Amy slowly closed the door behind him.

"I am *so* sorry, sweet cheeks," he said, simply oozing as much charm as he could. "I know I must have certainly puzzled you, but I have been *so* busy with work. I was called out of town unexpectedly and just didn't have the time or the chance to contact you."

She continued to look him squarely in the eye and maintained her stance.

"I have been gone up until just a few hours ago, and the very first thing I thought about was you. I just had to come see you right away. Please, please, please accept my apology. I am really and truly so, so sorry."

Amy unfolded her arms and gave the man a small smile.

Maybe Devon was mistaken about this handsome man, she thought.

Winston peeked around the corner from down the hallway to the back rooms. He stood and glared at the man.

"Oh, Joe," Amy said when she saw Winston. "I'm sorry, I didn't forget about your fear. I wasn't expecting to see you here tonight. I'll lock Winston up in my guest room."

"No. Don't do that, Amy. That's not fair for the poor pup. Look, I brought him a treat and maybe he'll like me better."

He had been carrying a canvas tote that had a bottle of wine, a corkscrew and a piece of partially cooked meat wrapped in wax paper. He had also been carrying a large bouquet of flowers.

"First, sweet cheeks, these are for you. I know you love flowers."

He handed Amy the bouquet and then he pulled out the wax paper and carefully opened it.

Winston sniffed the air and took a small step into the room.

"Maybe it's best if you hand it to him, Amy. I think he still might have some reservations about me, you know? He can probably still sense my fear. I'm trying to conceal it, really and truly I am."

Amy laid the bouquet momentarily on a coffee table. She then lifted the petite filet mignon daintily off the wax paper and headed toward Winston. The dog took another step toward the treat. His nose started actively twitching as he stepped again to get a closer sniff. His neck leaned in closer to the meat, continuing to sniff. His beautiful brown eyes glanced up into Amy's eyes and then, very carefully, he gently took the meat in his teeth and trotted off back down the hallway.

Goodbye, Winston, the assassin thought to himself.

"I've taught him to take his treats like a gentleman, and not be such an eager beaver," Amy laughed. "Let me put these flowers in a vase, Joe, and I'll be right back."

"Bring a couple of glasses with you, Amy. I brought another bottle of that wine that we never got to drink when I was here last time."

Amy was still apprehensive but he smelled *so* good, and he is so nicely dressed. A true gentleman.

Her defenses were down.

A few minutes later she came back from the kitchen with two glasses.

"I'm surprised that Winston hasn't come bouncing back in looking for more of that steak," she laughed. "It smelled so good I wanted to chomp on it myself!"

Richard Fleming chuckled.

"Maybe after our wine I could take you out for a real steak dinner. Not the puppy portion."

He pulled the bottle of wine from the tote and reached back in to get the corkscrew.

Amy watched as he adroitly uncorked the bottle and then he slowly removed the cork from the utensil, laying it on the coffee table in front of the sofa. He smiled at her as he could feel it beginning. His erection.

He poured the two glasses of wine as she held hers out to him and he held his.

"To us," the assassin said as he clinked his glass with hers. "A new beginning. A night to remember."

Amy wasn't so sure. Yet.

"We're just beginning to get to know each other, Joe," Amy smiled coyly. "I'm not sure how far this might go. You seem to disappear before we can *really* get to know each other."

"How far do you *want* to go, Amy?" Richard Fleming asked, his erection growing.

Amy wondered what she was doing. Was she egging him on to something a bit more dangerous? Who *is* this man?

"A step at a time, Joe. That's all. I seem to play things a bit cautiously now. I've been burned in the past."

"Aw, Amy...that's a shame. A nice kid like you? I can't believe that. Hey, can I use your bathroom for a minute. I suddenly have a call from nature, you know what I mean?"

Amy giggled. She pointed down the hall.

"Second door on the left. Don't let Winston scare you if he comes storming out of my bedroom."

"No problem," said the assassin. "Drink up and refill our glasses when I'm gone. Let's have some fun."

Richard Fleming closed the door to the bathroom and glanced at himself in the small mirror over the basin. He winked at himself. He slowly took off his nice sport jacket, folding it, and laid it on the edge of the tub. He slowly unbuttoned his shirt, sliding it off his shoulders revealing his smooth chest and the two tattoos. He unbuckled his trousers, dropping them to the floor. He stepped out of them, folding them neatly as well placing them on top of his jacket. He then slipped off his shoes and socks. He flushed the toilet so Amy wouldn't get too suspicious by his long absence. He dropped his boxers to the floor and stood up, looking down at his rigid erection in all its masculine glory.

38

Richard Fleming opened the bathroom door and briskly walked back into the living room.

Amy was sitting on the sofa still drinking her wine and let out a startled gasp when she saw him, dropping the glass on the floor where it shattered.

The naked assassin leaped on top of her, covering her mouth so she couldn't scream. She thrashed trying to get him off of her. She bit his hand making him momentarily free her face. She tried to raise her index finger and thumb to her lips to let out that shrill, familiar whistle to Winston but he grabbed her hands once again.

She gasped in fear and confusion when she saw the two swastika tattoos on his chest that were now mere inches from her face. She felt his erect penis as it thrust against her waist. He was trying to slide his body upwards, now bringing his erection in line with her chin.

Her fear turned to anger and then to disgust when she saw the bold tattoo SUCK THIS on his belly just above his pubic hair.

Not a chance, asshole, she thought as she struggled and continued to twist and turn.

His elbow was jabbing her in the ribs as he grabbed both her hands with his right hand, reaching toward the coffee table with his left. He was trying to find the corkscrew and it was just slightly out of his reach.

Her right hand slipped free and she hurriedly whistled.

But nothing. No response.

No Winston.

The assassin quickly grabbed her arms again with his right hand as his left found purchase with the corkscrew.

He leaned in very close, nose-to-nose with his victim and smirked. She smelled his now sour breath. Obviously he had been smoking before his arrival.

The loathsome man whispered into her ear.

"I hate to tell you, but your dog is probably dead by now. Or soon will be. And just for the record, sweet cheeks, my name ain't Joe. Just plain or otherwise. But you can take this information straight to heaven with you right now. My name is Richard Fleming. Give my regards to Jesus when you get there, will ya, you stupid twat!"

Although he used several aliases, he had never, *ever* told anyone his real name. A confession he would ultimately regret.

The tip of the corkscrew touched her on the forehead. He had her pinned down with the weight of his body. She could barely move. She could hardly breathe. Her anger returned to abject fear. She began again to thrash around trying to get the assassin off. Her frantic movements were making things difficult for him to get a grip on the corkscrew, but he did. She tried to scream as Fleming started to twist, but she couldn't utter a sound. Her voice was frozen in fear. What the hell was going on? Why was he doing this? She couldn't get her arms free as much as she tried. He was just too strong.

Suddenly Amy felt the sofa bounce and shift unexpectedly.

And the assassin screamed.

Bounding out of the bedroom like he was chasing a squirrel, Winston had finally responded to Amy's whistle by leaping on top of Fleming, biting him ferociously on the buttocks and shaking without loosening his grip.

The corkscrew went flying.

Amy abruptly sat upright.

Richard Fleming leaped up from the sofa, buttocks bleeding, as the dog came at him again. The assassin stepped on a piece of the shattered wine glass and it sliced into his heel.

"Get the stick, Winston!" Amy screamed. In a panic, that was all she could think of to yell. "Get the stick!"

The dog was momentarily confused. The only stick-like thing that Winston could see was a flopping penis, still surprisingly erect. He snarled at the naked man.

"No!" screamed Fleming as he grabbed his crotch for protection.

Growling ferociously the dog made a lunge, bumping into the coffee table, knocking over the wine bottle, as the assassin made a mad scramble bolting for the front door, slamming it behind him.

Amy, still trembling, dashed for the door locking it firmly and pulling the security chain across. She leaned up against the door, gasping for breath and almost in tears.

Richard Fleming was standing naked, sweaty, and bleeding in the hallway on the other side of the door.

Amy ran to her bedroom to call for the police.

In the hallway she barely missed stepping on the entire piece of petite filet mignon, uneaten and now covered in a fresh pile of dog shit.

Good dog! Smart dog. The nose knows!

Richard Fleming was nowhere to be found when the men from Scotland Yard showed up fifteen minutes later. But his bloody footprints could be seen on the hallway carpet leading into the fire escape stairwell.

39

In case of extenuating circumstances, Richard Fleming always kept a spare key to his Maserati in a small, magnetized box under its rear bumper. He had just never driven the vehicle while naked before. Running and dodging from tree to tree, and shrub to shrub keeping hidden in the shadows, he made a frantic, painful, mad dash from Amy's apartment across the car park and hurriedly got inside his car before being spotted by anyone. His ass was sore and bleeding. His foot was sore and bleeding. And he was raving mad. His life seemed to be unraveling. His prowess as a successful assassin was in tatters.

At least it was a dark, overcast night. No moonlight as he drove through the streets cautiously avoiding the busy areas. Although a car like his always seemed to attract attention, he was hoping that pedestrians had other thoughts on their minds at this hour. It had begun to rain, which was in his favor, and people on the streets huddled under their umbrellas.

He kept a key to his apartment in the glove box. If only he could make another mad dash from his car and get safely inside without being spotted and reported as a naked pervert exposing himself to the unsuspecting public.

He had multiple passports and now, with all of his plans gone wrong, *horribly* wrong, he would escape the country and disappear somewhere else on this planet.

But, as we all know, sometimes plans go awry.

———————

Still in shock and trembling, Amy had called the Metropolitan Police to report the incident and was a little surprised when men from Scotland Yard showed up. She was trying to maintain her composure as much as possible, urging back the tears that were just on the surface ready to burst forth. The two officers from Scotland Yard were polite and compassionate. She still had a small red mark on her forehead from the corkscrew and her muscles were sore from trying everything she could to thwart the strong assassin's attempt to kill her. Winston sat protectively by her side after being petted by the two dog-friendly men and having his ears ruffled.

"A horrible thing, ma'am," said one of the officers, notebook in hand. "Horrible. Please forgive me, but I must ask. I don't want to make any rash judgments here, but this just wasn't a lover's quarrel gone berserk, was it now?" And he smiled.

Amaryllis Cormier was taken aback by the question but understood that it *had* to be asked. She knew that things like this must happen all the time. Lover's quarrels, that is. *Not* frightening murder attempts.

Looking the man squarely in the eye she answered with a calm voice.

"Actually, officer, I hardly knew this man. We had a couple of… mmm…*strange* dates, if you will. He seemed to come on strong, then disappear for weeks on end. Claiming that business took him out of town. At first he told me his name was Joe. Just plain Joe, he said. Then he told me his name was Joe Richards. As he was trying to kill me he taunted me by telling me his name was Richard Fleming. I have no idea what the hell his name really is. I have no idea, now, who the hell *he* is!"

The two officers glanced at each other.

"Could you describe him for us, ma'am," said one of the men as he put pen to paper.

Amy thought for a moment. She was trying to get the image of his naked body out of her mind.

She cleared her throat.

"He is about a couple inches taller than my height, really. I'm 5' 7". I don't know how you say that here in the U.K. I couldn't even make a guess as to his weight. He has dark blond hair, maybe you might call it light brownish. He's very muscular but in a trim, toned way, I guess. He has a couple of disgusting tattoos. He's...you're going to think I'm just a silly woman...he's very handsome. Almost breathtaking. And he always smells so nice. He must wear a very expensive cologne or after shave."

The two officers once again looked at each other. This time with a different reason.

"Young lady, I don't want to alarm you any more than you've been...well, more than just a while ago. Scotland Yard investigated a brutal attack on a gentleman a couple nights ago over near the Regents Canal. The description of his assailant seems to match what you just told us."

The other officer reached into the pocket of his uniform and pulled out a folded piece of paper.

"The gentleman who was attacked gave us a very precise, detailed description about the man's face and we had our artist draw up the perpetrator according to that description. Does this look anything like your Richard Fleming?"

He unfolded a copy of the artist's sketch and held it up for Amy to see.

Her hands went straight to her mouth. She jolted in her seat and let out such a loud sudden gasp that Winston stood up and barked.

"Jesus Christ," said Amy, now with tears flowing. "That's him. That's definitely him!"

And then she remembered something. Something *extremely* important.

"Oh, my god, how stupid" she gasped. "How could I have forgotten *this* little thing?"

The officers stared at her, waiting for the next statement.

"I told you he attacked me after he had taken off all his clothes. He was naked when he came out of my bathroom. After Winston saved my life Joe…or…Fleming bolted for the door. His clothes are still there! Maybe even a wallet with identification. If it's real, that is, and not forged."

"Well then, ma'am," said the older of the two officers. "Don't touch a thing. You didn't did, you?"

Amy shook her head vigorously.

"And he touched that wine bottle that's lying under the coffee table…oh, and obviously that corkscrew that's over there on the rug," she answered. "I didn't even pick up the broken wine glass on the floor."

"We shall package up the lot and we're sure to get some decent fingerprints off of everything."

He wanted to be very careful how he phrased his next comments. He was cognizant of female sensibilities (he had five daughters) and was afraid she might faint dead away.

"I think…I *hope* that I can make a fairly honest evaluation here, young lady, and I wish not to frighten you any more than you have been already this evening. We have fingerprints and a weapon from the violent and nearly deadly crime committed two nights ago. If the fingerprints from tonight's heinous attack match those, then you may have helped break the case of a crime spree that's plagued all of Europe for the past few years. At least given us more evidence than we ever have had up until now to point our sights on the perpetrator."

Amy stopped crying and stared in disbelief.

"Why? How? What do you mean?"

"Dastardly, violent and incredibly ugly murders we...and also INTERPOL...believe have been committed by a highly skilled professional sex-crazed assassin. It now seems evident that he is your Richard Fleming."

If Amy hadn't been already seated she would have fallen down.

She and the two men conversed for ten more minutes before they left; telling her to make certain her door was firmly locked and bolted. They thanked her for the valuable information regarding the miscreant, tipped their hats and left the building.

Winston came over to her side, nudging under her hand, begging to be petted. She wrapped her arms around her four-legged protector, hugging him closely as the floodgates opened and she sobbed uncontrollably.

Amaryllis Cormier had survived a savage, almost deadly attack but the damage was done. It was a night she would never...*could* never forget.

40

Devon Stone, aware of the attack on Clovis James but oblivious to the horrendous attack on Amaryllis Cormier the night before, boarded the Flying Scotsman at Kings Cross Station. It was a beautiful morning and he was looking forward to the relaxing trip. It had been several years since he last rode this train.

There were twelve carriages that the magnificent steam engine would be pulling, two of which were 1st and 2nd class dining cars branded as "Restaurant Car". Devon avoided the carriage designated as "Women's Salon" which, actually, was a beauty salon for discriminating passengers. He found his spot for the journey in the carriage whose interior resembled a plush living room. Comfortable sofas and chairs in a soft pale green fabric, burgundy-colored carpets, overhead lighting and sconces lined the teakwood-paneled walls. Large potted palms were interspersed among the elegant furniture. All he needed now was a gin and tonic, but he would wait for a while. He knew a server would be along to take his request once the train was underway.

Lydia Hyui reacted with horrified shock when Amy called to tell her about the previous night's attack. Amy apologized profusely, but said she definitely would *not* be able to be at the bookstore today.

"My god, Amy!" Lydia responded. "There is no need for *you* to be apologizing. I can't believe this. You just made my skin crawl. I can't even imagine what it must have been like for you."

Amy fought back the tears once again as she explained the occurrence. And by whom.

"Wait," Lydia said, "this is the same young man who was so eager to meet Devon Stone?"

"Yes, Lydia, that sure was the goddamn bastard. Sorry for my language."

There was a moment of contemplative silence.

"Do you suppose there could be a connection? I mean, as to why he was so interested in Devon?"

"Frankly, I don't know. Joe…or Richard…or whatever the hell his name really is attacked another man a couple nights before me. I don't know if there was a connection there or not."

"Do you know who that other victim was?"

"No," answered Amy, "the officer from Scotland Yard never mentioned his name."

Lydia Hyui thought for a moment before speaking again.

"Stay home Amy. Take as long as you need. No need to rush back here. You have suffered a trauma that is unfathomable. Keep your door locked. Keep Winston by your side. I shall call Devon as soon as we hang up. Maybe he has a clue."

The call ended and Lydia Hyui dialed Devon Stone's telephone number.

The phone just rang and rang with no answer.

After twenty rings Lydia hung up. She would try again in an hour.

When she got no answer then, and in the several other attempts throughout the day she became concerned. Greatly concerned.

Richard Fleming's telephone started ringing practically after dawn. He knew, of course, who it would be.

"Fuck off, you little pygmy!" he yelled into the receiver before slamming it down.

The phone instantly began to ring again.

He picked up the receiver, slammed it back down again, then picked it up one more time and laid it on its side on the table.

What the bloody hell? Darrin Rand thought when the phone went dead.

He was calling the assassin to alert him to the fact that a sketch artist's rendering looking exactly like him was blasted on the front page of the morning papers. And announcing to the world his name.

An hour into the journey and Devon Stone was having difficulty concentrating on his writing. The small typewriter sat on his lap, momentarily untouched, as he continued to gaze out of the passing landscape. Little village after little village interspersed with beautiful, lush countryside. Green hedgerows and then bluebells, primroses and twinflower peeping out amongst the woodlands. Rivers, valleys, rolling hills…a true bucolic pleasure to see as the scenery changed from northern England eventually to southern Scotland. The train would make several stops along the way, gaining and dispersing passengers at each little station.

Devon would nod a greeting every once in a while when other passengers would saunter by possibly on the way to the restaurant car. Shortly after noontime a server came by, took Devon's order, and returned five minutes later with the first gin and tonic of the day. Several more would probably follow before reaching Edinburgh.

The early morning London, Paris, and Edinburgh newspapers

were placed at various tables through this car for the varied passengers.

Devon Stone did not notice the London newspaper with an article on the front page including a sketch artist's rendering of a sadistic assassin still on the loose.

41

The train arrived in Edinburgh even a few minutes ahead of schedule. Devon Stone, taking his time to disembark, took a leisurely stroll to his hotel a short walk away. It was a beautiful late afternoon and, despite the several spirited beverages he had consumed on the journey and a few interruptions to chat with a passenger or two, he was pleased with the progress he had made on his latest book. He was using the working title of *Murder By Proxy*. He had actually typed several pages during which he committed a murder. With the written word, that is. He chuckled to himself as he did so. His villain was a dastardly financial advisor with some devious, diabolical methods. He had Darrin Rand in mind when he created this particular character. Except that *this* scoundrel was better looking. And taller.

After checking in at the very gothic, very dark front desk of The Witchery, Devon Stone was led up to his room by a regal looking bellman. His suite, the Vestry, was reached by climbing a stone turret stairway up to the second floor. Devon did a double take when he was ushered into the lavish and spacious room. Silk-upholstered walls, a huge bateau bed with a fringed canopy, and three large windows overlooking The Royal Mile.

"Enjoy your stay, Mr. Stone," said the elderly bellman making a slight bow. "By the by, sir, I shall look forward to your book signing at the Old Town Bookshop tomorrow. Your books rival those of your friend Miss Christie if you care for my opinion. Perhaps one of our rumored ghosts might come to pay you a visit whilst you're here. I must say, and perhaps you shall agree, this hotel is just ripe for a great murder mystery." And he winked at Devon.

Devon Stone laughed and handed the man a £20 note.

"Oh, my! Thank you, sir. You are so gracious."

"See you tomorrow then, my good man," answered the author.

He glanced around the room again and was pleased that Christian de Lindsay and Dartmouth Press, his publishing house, had selected this intriguing hotel. *A great place for a murder mystery, indeed,* he thought to himself. *I must work it into my latest plot somehow.*

<hr/>

Drew Devereaux was getting frustrated and more than a bit nervous. Communication between the U.K. and Viet Nam was virtually nonexistent. After numerous tries, and several days, her contact at *LIFE* Magazine had finally been able to locate her position and sent a message via MARS (The U.S. Army's Military Auxiliary Radio System) to the rear-echelon group nearest to her. The cryptic message simply stated *Return home to London ASAP.*

She tried to contact Francine Quinn, her assistant, both at the photo studio and then at her home to find out any news. Why the urgent order to return home? Was something seriously dangerous about to happen? *What could be more dangerous than World War II?* Drew thought. The calls had to go through multiple switchboards and volunteer HAM operators. It was time consuming and when there were no answers at either number, Drew tried to get in touch with Devon Stone. Again, without success. She kept trying at different times throughout the day and night. Now she became *really* worried.

"We're all pullin' out, ma'am," the American army officer said to her after she asked. "That's all I can tell ya. We shouldn't have been here to begin with in my honest opinion, but please don't ya quote me on that."

She made her arrangements to get back to London as soon as she could. But it would be a long, tedious, and potentially dangerous journey to do so.

Devon Stone took a refreshing bath in an old claw-foot tub after his long day on the train, changed into evening attire, deciding to check the acclaimed hotel's restaurant.

He was just as impressed with the massive dining room as he was with his room upstairs. Dark wood paneling with centuries-old hand carved medieval-looking motifs from floor to ceiling topped off by a carved oak leaf crown molding. The ceiling overhead was just as impressive, also totally dark oak wood with deep-set hexagonal panels from end to end. Tri-light sconces lined the walls and tall candelabras on every table.

Well, thought a smiling Devon Stone as he entered the room to be greeted by a tuxedoed maître d', *this will surely set Dartmouth Press back a shilling or two. I shall go big! I'm worth it.*

No sooner had he been seated and handed an extensive menu when a tuxedoed waiter appeared by his table.

"Good evening, Mr. Stone," he said with a broad, friendly smile. "It shall be a distinct pleasure serving you, sir. And, I might add, it will be a thrill for both my wife and I to greet you at the book signing tomorrow."

Good grief, thought Devon Stone, *I must have an entire fan club working at this hotel.*

"Well, thank *you,* sir," answered Devon.

The waiter bowed. "May I bring you a spirited beverage to start the meal off properly? I say spirited, sir, because this place is haunted as you may know."

Devon thought for a moment.

"I rarely drink spirits," he said with a chuckle and a wink, "but let's start off with your finest gin and a splash of tonic."

Two minutes later a tuxedoed barman returned with the beverage.

"Thank you," Devon said to the man. "Please keep them coming until it looks as though I might fall out of my seat."

Devon perused the menu and he knew in an instant that it would be very difficult to decide.

Eventually he did so, and throughout the evening he dined on Baked Hand-Dived Orkney Scallops for a starter, Loin of Glenfeshie Venison for his entrée and a Forced Yorkshire Rhubarb Custard Tart with rhubarb ice cream for dessert. Somewhere early on in his meal he switched from gin and tonics to a bottle of Domaine Trapet Marsannay, a red burgundy, downing the entire bottle.

Christian de Lindsay will certainly soil his trousers when he gets the invoice for this little excursion, Devon chuckled to himself.

He did not yet fall out of his seat although the room was beginning to look a bit hazy.

Two hours later he had barely been in bed for ten minutes when he heard a strange sound in his room. Someone or something was moving, shuffling about. At first he thought that the sound had come from under his bed. It was dark but he had kept the thick draperies on the windows open. There was moonlight outside and it shone onto the floor. Something bumped the bed. Suddenly a silhouette appeared standing up at the foot of his bed. It was a man. A small man.

42

Not knowing if Darrin Rand had really been wily enough to follow him today, Devon Stone had his pistol on the nightstand next to his bed just in case. He cautiously reached for it, holding it poised to be fired if the figure made a threatening move. The short silhouette inched his way around the foot of the bed, heading toward Devon. All of a sudden the figure lifted what looked like a long sword or a spear of some kind in his hand, ready to strike. Devon waited no longer. He fired the pistol at the figure, shattering one of the large windows directly behind the man as the glass shards came falling down, tinkling loudly to the hardwood floor.

Devon Stone jolted upright and gasped out loud, his heart rate racing. He rapidly blinked his eyes and shook his head. It was still dark. Very dark. He reached over and switched on the little light that was on his nightstand. The draperies covering the windows were drawn tightly closed. No moonlight streaming onto the floor. In fact, it had been raining and there was a distant rumble of thunder. No window had been shattered. His pistol, unfired, was still laying on the nightstand by his bed. And he was alone in his room.

Bloody fucking hell, he thought, *either too much wine and gin...or one of the Witchery's ghosts just came to call.*

He lay back in his bed, soon falling into a shallow sleep once again. But first he had moved his pistol to under his pillow.

Amaryllis Cormier tossed and turned in her rumpled sheets for hours. Even with Winston up on the bed with her she still felt nervous and vulnerable. She had never owned, nor even fired a gun of any kind in her life but she was seriously thinking of getting one. When she eventually fell asleep she dreamed of shooting off a very private part of just plain Joe.

———⟫●⟪———

Richard Fleming packed his bags and was ready to depart for the airport. He spoke fluent French; therefore he would be using his faked French passport with the name Francoise Richard. Discovering earlier in the day that his image was probably now seen by a vast majority of Englanders, he resorted to his makeup kit and an effective disguise. He dyed his hair black, created a fake mustache and wore thin wire-rimmed glasses, now matching his passport photograph. He found an old cane in the back of his closet and he practiced walking with a pronounced limp. His foot was still sore from stepping on the broken wine glass so it wasn't too much of a fake limp.

However, he would soon discover that it was all for naught.

Waiting until long after dark to leave, he quietly left his apartment and headed to the building's underground car park.

But someone was waiting for him back in the shadows. Someone who had expected him to make an escape. Someone who knew just about all of Fleming's disguises from the past. Someone who was not very happy.

Richard Fleming was within a few feet of his car when he heard a gunshot from behind him. Instantly he felt a burning, painful sensation in his right leg and he crumpled to the ground, shocked and surprised. His cane and wire-rimmed glasses went sailing across the concrete floor.

His ass was still extremely sore from a dog bite, and now this.

"You're a bloody idiot," said Darrin Rand as he slowly approached the fallen man. "I might be challenged in height, but I'm certainly no pygmy."

The assassin tried to turn over but it was painful to do so.

"You fucked up, Fleming," said Rand with an evil glint in his eye. "For a world-class assassin, my friend, you're slipping. No, you slipped. For probably the first time in your murdering life you left a witness. And one who can identify you. And now they know your name. That's unfortunate, isn't it? This time you fucked up big time."

Fleming simply stared in disbelief at the little man.

"You have a gorgeous apartment in Athens. Thanks for showing it off to me. I'm going to enjoy it. I can't drive either of your fancy cars but, what the hell, eh?"

"What the *hell* are you talking about, Rand?"

Darrin Rand shrugged his shoulders.

"I know your secrets, my friend, and…well, unfortunately, you know mine. All of Europe is now on the lookout for your handsome face. And you'll probably soon be caught. I can't have that now, can I? You'll probably be forced to reveal certain details, eh? No denying it, you will. You have served me well in the past, my dear Richard, but apparently you can no longer be relied upon."

"What the f…"

Richard Fleming neither heard the gunshot nor felt the bullet as it entered his forehead.

43

Considering the unexpectedly unusual night Devon Stone had just experienced he vowed that he would restrict his liquid intake for the remainder of his stay in Edinburgh to nothing stronger than tea or coffee. Witchery ghosts and dreams be damned!

He had a book signing event today; from 1 P.M. until 4 P.M., and he wanted to be alert and as friendly as possible. He remembered such events here in Scotland before and the attendees seemed to be inquisitive, polite, sometimes talkative, sometimes a bit brash, but always rewarding with the sale of dozens more books.

Bathed and dressed, at 10 A.M. he sat at the same table he had the night before and awaited his ordered first coffee of the day. The young waiter brought him the late morning edition of the *London Times* for his pleasure before his breakfast was delivered. He hardly paid attention to the blaring banner headline, in all bold capital letters.

HUNTED ASSASSIN FOUND SLAIN!

I spend most of my time, Devon thought, *writing murders. I don't need to read about them in the press as well.*

Even the accompanying sketch artist's rendering of the assassin didn't draw much of his attention. It meant nothing to him.

Obviously the hunted assassin wasn't Darrin Rand, as he could tell by the sketch. He simply wasn't interested.

Even assassins aren't safe from assassins anywhere anymore, he chuckled to himself.

He was more intrigued reading about the phenomenon of the dangerous typhoon Sarah that had been approaching the Philippines, changing direction at the last moment, and then dissipating. An article about a volcano in Russia's Kamchatka Peninsula erupting drew his attention next.

Nature at her finest, he thought. *We'll never be able to control it.*

He was about to turn the page when something just happened to catch his eye. It was a name. Clovis James. It was in that article about the slain assassin.

And *then* he started to read the entire article.

———⟫●⟪———

Clovis James had been awakened earlier by his telephone ringing at 7 A.M.

"Mr. James," said a deep male voice, which the critic didn't recognize, "I'm so sorry to disturb you at this early hour. This is Chief Inspector Downing from Scotland Yard."

"Good morning, Inspector," answered a groggy Clovis James. "I'm no less grumpy at this hour than any other. The meaning of your call is what, sir?"

"Based upon early observation, apparently it looks as though your attacker from those nights ago was, himself, murdered late last night."

A moment of stunned silence.

"I didn't do it," the critic blurted out.

———⟫●⟪———

Devon Stone nearly dropped his coffee cup when he read about the attack several days ago of the drama critic, of which he was fully aware. The article mentioned another attack by the same perpetrator but didn't give the name of the young female victim to protect her privacy.

What about the critic, Devon thought, *doesn't he deserve privacy as well?*

His breakfast was delivered but he was no longer hungry.

He called his waiter to the table.

"I'm so sorry, lad," he said, "I must hasten back to my room immediately. Please have someone bring my breakfast to my room. Room 222, the Vestry. I apologize profusely for the inconvenience."

He handed the young waiter a £10 note and ran from the room.

Chief Inspector Downing gave a little nervous chuckle.

"No, sir, I didn't imagine for a second that you did the man in. I wouldn't have blamed you, of course. I just wanted to ease your mind so you can rest easier and not fear for a return visit from the blighter. I'm sure, sir, that your own newspaper will be covering the story but I wanted to alert you myself. INTERPOL will be closing out their Red Notice on the bast…, I mean gentleman, but they will more than likely be opening a new one on this latest killer. I feel certain that this was *not* a random killing or attempted mugging gone wrong. This man had enemies."

"Thank you, Inspector," responded the critic, "I certainly *do* appreciate this call."

Amaryllis Cormier couldn't believe her eyes when she read the morning newspaper. She gasped loudly, making Winston hurry to her side. She gently stroked him on his head.

She was relieved and elated...but...

Who killed him? Amy thought. *And why?*

⊷●⊶

Clovis James had lay awake for the past hour or so following the surprise call from Scotland Yard. He was nearly asleep when the telephone rang again.

"Jesus fucking Christ!" he blurted out loud as he threw back the bed covers.

"Hello?" he said impatiently upon answering the phone.

"Please tell me that you didn't do it," was all that was said by an anxious Devon Stone.

44

"Blast it, Stone! If I could have, I would have," Clovis James practically yelled into the receiver. "But I think we both might have an idea who may have done the deed."

"Correct you are, my friend," answered Devon Stone. "I can't imagine that INTERPOL does *not* have a Red Notice out on Darrin Rand, but we must alert them in any event. Chester and Fiona might still have better connections at this point."

"You're still in Edinburgh, I assume," said the critic. "I'll contact both Chester and Fiona at a more decent hour for civilized people to be up and about."

Devon Stone glanced at his watch.

"It's 10:35, Clovis. *You're* up."

"I said *civilized* people, Stone. Civilized people. Among which I am not, apparently."

───────◆───────

Four hours later Devon Stone was halfway through his first book-signing event on this trip. He was smiling graciously, answering questions, allowing photographs to be taken, being practically blinded by the flash bulbs, and signing so many books that his wrist was beginning to hurt.

This morning's news and the conversation with Clovis James never left his mind, however. He was more certain than ever that there was a connection between Darrin Rand and the recently murdered assassin. But how and why?

Two other unsettling pieces of news lay ahead for the author. Devon was still unaware of the traumatizing attack on Amaryllis Cormier and the murder of Francine Quinn, Drew Devereaux's assistant.

Maude Landis, the publisher's mother (a saint if ever there was one), was aghast when she read the morning's newspaper. She was in a tizzy when she reached for the phone.

"Christian," she said breathlessly as her telephone call was put through to his office. "Christian. Did you read about that *awful* critic being attacked by that murdered scoundrel? What sort of people do you associate with?"

"Yes, I read it. He's *not* an awful critic, Mother, only a stringent one. And we only went to the races with him. Once. That's all. I do *not* associate with him."

Christian de Lindsay pictured his mother now clutching her pearls and about to faint.

"Relax, Mother, I seriously doubt that neither you nor I are being stalked by a crazed murderer. But thank you very much for putting that thought into my head!"

Devon Stone was correct. Christian de Lindsay *was* a nervous Nelly.

He then left a message with the Witchery Hotel operator in Edinburgh to have Devon Stone contact him at his convenience.

"No, Christian, neither you nor your mother have anything to be concerned about," Devon said, trying to assuage any fears that his now more nervous than ever publisher might have. "Why would you even think that?"

He did *not* want to bring up his own and the critic's connection to the loose cannon named Darrin Rand. "I do believe that the brutal attack on Clovis was a random attempted robbery gone wrong. Besides, you both met him only once. So calm down."

There was silence on the other end of the line. Devon waited. But, apparently, the obvious question wasn't forthcoming.

"The event up here went well today, by the way, Christian, thanks for asking," Devon finally said with a modicum of sarcasm. "You should be very pleased. My royalties shall be a great reward. Perhaps I *shall* purchase that Jackson Pollock after all."

He was trying to make light of the situation but he *knew* that there still was the potential for danger ahead for him.

———◦———

Darrin Rand was getting more frustrated by the hour. He had lost track of his target, Daniel Stein…Devon Stone…while he had been concentrating on tracking down and rashly killing the young assassin, Richard Fleming. He had disregarded not only caution but logic as well, for which he was now regretful. Why had he done that?

From now onward he had to rely upon his own well-trained abilities. His mind was reeling. His world was unraveling. His mental capacity was becoming undone, more and more irrational, although he wasn't yet aware of it.

———◦———

Today's event at the little bookshop was considered by Devon Stone to be a pleasant success. But he vowed to himself that there would be no repeat of last evening's gargantuan meal including way too many spirits, both the liquid kind and…well, whatever it was that had visited him in his room last night. Yes, it was a dream but the hotel was haunted nonetheless.

The cobblestone walkway that was the Royal Mile was still wet and slick from last evening's rain, reflecting the lights from the surrounding businesses. Several young and rowdy groups, laughing and chattering, were out and about possibly doing their nightly pub-crawls. Devon sauntered back toward the Witchery Hotel and passed the very spot outside of the pub where he had apprehended Darrin Rand more than a decade earlier. He stopped walking and the image of his tussle with the small man flashed through his mind.

Greyfriars Bobby Bar, named after a loyal Skye terrier who faithfully stood guard over his master's grave for fourteen years, seemed to have a magnetic pull on the author.

What the hell, he thought, *one little drink couldn't hurt.*

As he walked past the little bronze statue of the legendary dog out front, he petted it on the head and smiled.

I need a dog, he thought. *Someone who wouldn't judge my drinking habits.* And he chuckled.

He allotted himself one pint of Guinness, accompanied by a small steak pie. That was reasonable.

An hour later he was back in his room where he sat for another hour typing away on his newest book.

An hour after that he was sound asleep.

He was visited by neither ghost nor nightmare and awoke completely refreshed by daybreak.

PART THREE

UNDONE

The spring is wound up tight. It will uncoil of itself.
That is what is so convenient in tragedy. The least
little turn of the wrist will do the job.

Jean Anouilh - Antigone

45

Three mornings later Devon Stone awoke in his own bed, relieved that the successful journey to Edinburgh was now behind him.

But his sense of calm and relaxation would be short-lived.

A frantic Lydia Hyui had found out from Christian de Lindsay where Devon Stone had been and why he was unreachable at home. She was furious about the near-fatal attack on poor Amy.

After a long, tiring, circuitous trip back to England Drew Devereaux faced the devastating news of the fire at her studio and the murder of her long-time assistant and friend, Francine Quinn.

Two situations that went from bad to worse.

Two situations, both caused by the fact that Devon Stone had rattled the cage of the vile, evasive Country Mouse.

He had just set his feet on the floor and was about to rise from his bed when his doorbell rang. And rang. And rang once again.

"Bloody hell!" he said out loud.

He hastily straightened his pajamas, wrapped his dressing gown around him and, with rumpled hair and a days worth of stubble on his chin, he ran down the stairs.

Upon opening the front door a disgruntled Lydia Hyui stood on his small porch, arms folded across her chest, glowering at him.

"What the...?" he said as she pushed right past him and stood in his foyer.

With a confused look on his face, he slowly closed the door. It was obvious that the woman was disturbed about something but... what? She wasn't here for a little quick romantic encounter, which was made quite clear. That hadn't happened in several months. Perhaps even a year now.

Lydia Hyui unfolded her arms and seemed to relax.

"I'm sorry, Devon. I've been trying to contact you for days. Thanks to Christian I found out where you were. I thought the worst, considering."

Devon Stone shook his head. More confusion.

"Lydia, you have me at a loss. Considering *what*, exactly?"

"About *Amy*, of course. Considering what happened to her I thought that perhaps he had gotten *you*, too."

Devon simply stared at her.

"All right, Lydia. Let's start this conversation again at the beginning and tell me what the bloody hell you are talking about. What about Amy and who, exactly, might have gotten to me? Is Amy all right?"

They hadn't even left the foyer, but Lydia Hyui told Devon about the situation with Amy and the young man who attacked her.

"It's because of *you*, Devon. And because of Clovis James and that photograph at the exhibition. Amy told me all about it and what you're trying to do. To find some fiendish little man."

Devon Stone was aghast. So it was *Amy* who had been that unnamed female victim of the attack that had been mentioned in the newspaper article. He should have paid closer attention at the time.

"Stay for a while, Lydia, and let me digest this situation. I'll make some coffee...or tea?"

"No, Devon. Thanks. I just wanted to tell you in person. Evidently Amy's ruthless attacker was killed. But by whom? That little man you're trying to find? And is he trying to find you? Just be careful, Devon. Please."

With that, Lydia gave Devon a sweet, gentle kiss on the cheek and left.

He closed the door slowly behind her and stood there in silence. His day had just begun with a shock but it was about to get worse.

He was still reeling from the news from Lydia regarding Amy's violent, near-deadly attack as he was sipping his first cup of coffee when the telephone rang. He was hesitant to pick it up, but he did.

"Good morning, Devon," said Drew Devereaux.

46

The long, sad, disturbing telephone conversation with the photographer ended.

He felt angry. He felt guilty.

He made one more phone call, catching Lydia Hyui just as she had opened her bookshop and not long after she had left him speechless at his front door.

It had become a day for which he had not planned. *But the best laid plans of mice and men*, he thought, *often go awry*.

He made a quick telephone call to Fiona Thayer.

Another phone call, this time to Amaryllis Cormier. He had gotten Amy's number from Lydia.

And then he sat back thinking about setting a trap. A mousetrap. For a Country Mouse.

———————⊰⊱———————

Two hours later Devon Stone rang the doorbell to Amy's apartment. He was not alone.

Amy peered through her little peephole in her door and smiled when she saw Devon. She hastily opened the door and just as quickly hugged him so tightly he almost fell over backwards.

Fiona Thayer stood back and smiled.

"Oh, Devon," Amy said almost in tears. "I should have listened to your warning. I was *so* stupid. *So* oblivious. So…"

"Just be grateful, Amy," interrupted Devon, "that you're not *so* dead!"

Amy released her hold on Devon and then smiled at the lady who had been standing behind him.

"Amy, I brought a very good friend with me. Someone who went through a traumatic experience such as yours."

Before he could introduce Fiona, hearing Devon Stone's voice Winston came bounding out of a backroom somewhere and ran right up to Devon, wagging his tail and nudging him waiting to be petted. Dog lovers know that dogs smile and that is exactly what Winston was doing.

Fiona Thayer got a huge smile on *her* face as she bent down reaching for the dog.

"Oh, what a magnificent creature you are!" she said as Winston came to her for a greeting as well, tail wagging even faster. "And I understand that you are quite a hero at that. Well done. Well done."

She bent further down and Winston licked her face as she laughed.

"Winston, behave!" admonished Amy.

"Perfectly all right, my dear," responded Fiona. "Perhaps I should kiss him right back."

They all laughed at that.

"Amy, please let me introduce my dog-loving friend Fiona Thayer," Devon said, stepping aside so Fiona could take Amy's hand. "I brought her here for a reason. I just learned this morning of your horrible ordeal, for which I feel a bit guilty. More than a bit, actually. Fiona, years ago, suffered a great traumatic, life-threatening attack and..."

"Please, Devon," interrupted Fiona Thayer holding up her hand, "allow me to take it from here. Amy, dear, there's no need for me to go into details at this point, but I suffered great physical pain and dark emotional stress for a long time afterwards. I had some wonderful people helping me recover. My very good friend Devon, here, was one of them and he was very wise to ask for *my* help a few hours ago when he told me about your situation. I know only too well what is going through your poor young mind at the moment. The mind…and memory…can be dreadful places."

Amy started to cry.

"Please, let's all sit down," Amy said as she showed them to the chairs. Although it didn't register with Devon at first, Amy avoided sitting on the sofa.

"If you'll permit it, please let me be your guide," continued Fiona. "I can help you move down that very dark labyrinth so that you can, and *will* come out on the bright side of your horrible experience. Trust me, sweet Amy, you won't want to take that journey alone."

Amaryllis Cormier sat still for a moment, wiping away her tears with the back of her hand. Winston sat by her side, looking up into her face.

"I have no idea who you are, Fiona," Amy finally said after a big sigh and a partial sob. "I just met you moments ago. But…can I give you a great big hug right now?"

———————⊰●⊱———————

The following afternoon Devon Stone and Drew Devereaux sat side by side up on Devon's rooftop. It had been an unusually warm day and the pleasant air was refreshing. They each were sipping cups of tea. Chester Davenport had tried out a new cookie recipe earlier in the day…with his secret ingredient…and had brought some over for Devon to sample.

When Drew had first learned of her damaged studio and murdered friend upon arriving home from Viet Nam she felt utterly bereft. The more she thought about it, her feelings turned to anger. This whole sorrowful scenario had happened because of Devon

Stone. One very little man in Devon's past. And one photograph. One coincidence after the other had led to Francine's death. She did not know, now, where their relationship might go. Would she hold Devon Stone responsible forever?

As they sat and sipped, Devon slowly doled out pieces of information regarding his involvement with the war. Drew Devereaux was instantly fascinated by the revelation regarding Devon's past with MI5.

"You've been more than tight-lipped about your past, Devon, up until now. I always had the suspicion that you were more than just an author."

"Just an author?" Devon reacted with a jolt. "*Just* an author?"

She snickered and took another sip of her tea.

They both watched a flock of homing pigeons swoop low overhead and come to roost on the roof next door.

"So, what was it with the strange, evil little man, Devon? What was *his* history?"

Devon Stone sat back in contemplation before he spoke.

"He was a conundrum right from the start. Unfortunately those of us at MI5 and those at MI6 missed certain…now obvious…clues. Due diligence was sorely lacking, but it was wartime. He was a good man, until he wasn't."

"Why, then, was he a *hunted* man? What caused him to kill your friend's uncle?"

Devon sighed, shaking is head.

"This will sound more bizarre as I go along. Bear with me, my dear. Darrin Rand, despite his affliction, his diminutive size if you will, had a ravenous sexual appetite. It played right into a crazy program initiated by Adolph Hitler himself."

Drew Devereaux reacted with a stunned look on her face.

"Excuse me? What?"

Devon Stone laughed.

"I told you this would get bizarre. Yes, Hitler was aware that Germany's population had been declining and because of his successes in seizing territory at the beginning of the war he wanted to populate said territories with his own master race. Get ready, my dear, and here comes the insane part. A program was initiated within Germany rewarding women for having children. As many as possible. It was their *duty* to become baby factories for the Father Land, whether or not they were even married. Contraception was abandoned and abortions were illegal."

Drew Devereaux stared at Devon Stone in disbelief.

"You're making this up as you go along, aren't you, Devon?"

"Sadly, no. I may have a vivid imagination, DeeDee, but what I'm telling you is absolutely true. Darrin Rand was entrenched undercover at the time in Germany. He was a good...even great spy. He was a cunning assassin when the time came. He learned of Hitler's plan and his libido was turned on full force. He became a one-man seducing, raping machine. Of course, MI5 was not aware of his actions for quite a while."

"I assume, then, that his actions somehow eventually became known?" Drew asked, still bewildered by this strange tale.

"Yes, one cannot keep the news of a very small man attacking and raping women quiet for long, even in the midst of a violent war going on. Eventually German women spread the word themselves to be on the lookout for this pint-sized idiot. According to some unverified reports, Darrin Rand may have impregnated over thirty women...possibly even more. Shockingly, one poor girl was a mere thirteen years old. Aside from the abhorrent nature of his activity committed as a British subject, in his demented actions he was actually committing treason of sorts by playing into Hitler's reckless program."

"I simply cannot believe this, Devon. The man was evil reincarnate. Still is, evidently."

"From what Clovis and I were able to deduce, his uncle was about to report the finding to the higher ups in command. In desperation, Rand must have killed Alistair Wallace moments after you took that fateful photograph."

"But why, then, was Darrin Rand so intent on killing *you*? What did *you* have to do with him?"

"Ah, well. I'll skip ahead in time. Rand's actions *did* become known and he deserted his countrymen. He was a hunted man. Although it took some time, we eventually tracked him down, to Edinburgh of all places, and I was the one who captured him. Not without some painful resistance on his part. He was committed, for life, to a sanatorium for the criminally insane, which, of course, he was. He was a dangerous lunatic, pure and simple. The last I saw of him was there, at the sanatorium. And as I leaned over his bed, he was raging mad and vowed to kill me if it was the last thing he ever did. The murder of Devon Stone, ne Daniel Stein, was first and foremost on his deviant mind for the past dozen years or so."

"Who, then, do you suppose killed my poor Francine? Darrin Rand or that creep who attacked your friend Amy?"

Devon Stone clasped his two hands together behind his head, leaned back and stared up into space.

"If I were writing this plot," he began, "I'd say it was Rand. He probably knew of you but I doubt that Fleming did. He went to your studio to find you...perhaps to harm you or kidnap you to get at me...and found Francine instead. Somehow he must have surprised her. She knew about Rand, recognizing him, because of the story Clovis and I told you that day at your place. There may have been an altercation, he panicked and shot her. That sounds like an obvious scenario to me but then, I'm just an author."

Drew Devereaux didn't feel much like laughing, but she did anyway. Her mood and her feelings toward Devon Stone had once again softened.

"I don't know why, Devon, but I continually find you disarming. Right from the very beginning when we first met at my studio. Your just-revealed past? Wow! How exciting. Your present. Oh, my. Intriguing. Why are you *still* a bachelor?"

Devon Stone stopped staring into space and turned to look Drew Devereaux in her beautiful eyes.

"Because, my dear," he said, "I've just been waiting for *you*."

47

Devon Stone and Drew Devereaux awoke, side by side, in Devon's bedroom early the next morning. They smiled at each other and rolled over facing one another, then kissed. Rain was beating against the large windows and the sound soon lulled the two back into a blissful sleep. A Scotsman might say that they were hurkle-durkling. The trauma of the recent events for both of them was temporarily forgotten. Or, at least, shunted aside.

By the time they finally awoke again the rain had stopped, the noontime sun had broken through the clouds and bright light was streaming into the room. Devon got out of the bed and padded, naked, over to the window and drew the thick draperies closed, darkening the room once again.

"Oh, Devon. Please don't do that. I was enjoying the view."

"Of the top half of the house across the street?"

Drew Devereaux laughed.

"No, sweet man. The view was in here. I haven't seen too many naked authors lately."

⇒●⇐

An hour later they were just finishing their coffee and porridge as the sunlight continued to stream into the kitchen.

"I'm almost afraid to ask, Devon," Drew said with hesitation. "What comes next?"

"I do think that I shall bathe and shave," he answered with a smile.

"Oh, come on, Devon. Don't be coy. You know what I mean."

Devon sat back, sipping the last of the coffee in his cup.

"I do, indeed, DeeDee. Oh. That sounded funny, didn't it?"

Drew shook her head and rolled her eyes.

"I know that Rand knows where *I* live. The unfortunate thing is that I do not know where *that* rat has *his* hole. I've been thinking about the ways I can set a trap. He's very adroit about avoiding capture, so I must lure him out and then lure him into my trap. Obviously I've got to confront him in some manner to bring this deadly situation to a conclusion. And I'm seriously considering bringing someone else in to help."

"Me?" Drew asked incredulously.

"No, no, no. Of course not. I want you as far away from harm as possible. I'm thinking of asking someone who has a stake in the scenario that started this thing a few months back. Someone who has helped me before a few years ago. Someone who has absolutely no qualms about going a bit beyond the law."

<hr />

"Of course, I will, Stone," said Clovis James. "How could you have thought otherwise?"

48

Devon Stone and Clovis James sat at Devon's dining room table. A large map of Hampstead Heath lay out before them.

"It's going to be a matter of deception, my friend," Devon said. "Along with the game of chance and probability. And I shall be the distraction, if you will."

"I don't like it, Stone," answered the critic. *Always* the critic. "It sounds to me that you shall be walking straight into a sure deathtrap."

"I may be, but we need to draw the blighter out. Get this over with. Knowing the man as I do, he'll want to gloat over my impending death and shall not kill me outright by shooting me from afar. Frankly I'm surprised that he tried to shoot me from behind just outside the Holly Bush. He'll want to look me square in the eyes and watch me die up close. He'll want to taunt me...man to man. Face to face."

"Stone, you're an idiot. Let's rethink this one. Please!"

Drew Devereaux had been sitting at the far end of the table. Just listening. And thinking. She had a surprising idea.

"Devon," she spoke up, pursing her lips. "Hmm...I understand those old military tactics that you seem to be proposing. I've seen them in action. But this will be a different battlefield, of course, in a manner of speaking. Let me offer a few suggestions."

Darrin Rand was coming undone. His sanity was fighting an internal battle with the desire to murder his mortal enemy. He avoided daylight and traveled, as little as necessary, after dark.

Devon Stone had not left his house in days. Rand wasn't crazy enough to simply ring Stone's front doorbell and blast him to bits when he opened the door.

No. That was not even a plan to be considered.

He wanted to catch him unaware, outside somewhere, and watch him die, slowly, as Rand stood over him and laughed.

Darrin Rand did not know that Devon Stone had company. Nor did he know that there was a back entry, and exit, from Devon's house.

———⋙◉⋘———

It was barely dawn, a dark, cloudy day ahead. Darrin Rand had been hoping that sooner or later Devon Stone would *have* to leave his house.

Today was the day. He would now, at last, get his chance.

He had been hiding in his car a block away from Stone's house almost every day and night for a week. Leaving on short breaks for hygiene and dining reasons. He thought that his stealth had been unobserved.

He was mistaken.

Devon Stone opened his front door and blithely walked down the steps, turning toward Hampstead Heath when his feet hit the pavement. He then walked briskly up the street.

Darrin Rand had to be cautious, of course, because his size, even in the dim early morning light, would give him away should Stone chance to turn and look behind him.

Damn, Rand thought, *Stone's pace will kill me!*

Indeed, Devon Stone walked with a fast, determined stride.

Keeping a very safe distance, Rand could tell that Devon Stone appeared to be unarmed. At least he wasn't carrying any weapon that was visible. But where was he going at this hour...and why?

Twenty minutes later Darrin Rand was sweating profusely and the muscles in his short legs were on fire. But now he had to catch up.

Devon Stone had entered the Heath and was heading toward a stand of trees. One of them an old, decaying pedunculate oak. No one else was around.

Darrin Rand took out his concealed pistol and fired, making sure it hit the ground just to the right of Devon Stone, directly at his feet.

The gunshot frightened a flock of ravens that had been roosting in the trees and they took flight, calling angrily.

Devon Stone stopped walking, smiled, and slowly turned around as his nemesis slowly ambled up to him.

The two of them stood facing each other, now not more than ten feet apart.

Darrin Rand shook his head, glaring up at Devon Stone.

And Devon Stone looked down upon Darrin Rand.

"Well, well, well, just look at the two of us, Stone, Stein... whichever you are. *Whoever* you are. Here we are together again at last. Laughable, isn't it? David and Goliath." Sneered Darrin Rand.

"Ah, but don't you see the irony there, little man?" answered Devon with a broad grin.

"Irony? What are you talking about? What fucking irony?"

Devon folded his arms across his chest.

"If you happen to believe in that old fairy tale, Goliath was felled by a stone. Today, *David* will be felled by a Stone."

"Oh, no, you're wrong there, Stone. I told you years ago that I was going to kill you if it was the last thing I ever did. I'm going to love watching you bleed out in front of me. And, look...here *you* are. Unarmed and *oops*...I am not!"

Rand thought about it for a second too long and was just about to raise his pistol.

Action beats reaction.

With that, a gunshot rang out from behind the trees and Darrin Rand's hand, holding the firearm, was shattered. His right hand. His gun dropped.

"What the fuck!" he screamed in shock more than from pain. He tried to reach for the gun with his left hand, the prosthesis, but Devon Stone was too quick and he kicked it aside, out of reach.

"Someday, Rand, there will be a tomorrow that starts without me. But it shan't be tomorrow or the next. You, however, cannot say the same."

It still hadn't gotten light enough but Darrin Rand saw some sort of a shadowy figure move behind Devon Stone.

Drew Devereaux walked from behind the oak tree, a rifle in one hand, and a brand new camera hanging from a strap around her neck. She handed the rifle to Devon.

"Funny thing, isn't Rand? Although, I don't see you laughing. I just recently learned that this beautiful woman is a crack shot with more than just a camera. A regular Annie Oakley she is."

Darrin Rand was about to become even more undone.

"But I have a deal for you, my demented murderous friend. My suggestion to you right now, Rand," said Devon Stone with a snicker, "is that you start running. Run fast, little man. Run out of the Heath. Run back down to your car. *Here's* the deal. If you should make it there safely before I catch you, you'll be a free man. I shall walk slowly. No pun intended, considering your…current situation, but I've got to hand it to you. You've tracked *me* down before I could track *you* down. Run. I promise. I'll do nothing more. Go. Now!"

Drew Devereaux quickly held up her camera, pointing it at Rand and began shooting with her new electronic strobe, one flash after the other, blinding the little man at first and frightening him even more. He backed up, nearly stumbling as he did so.

Darrin Rand was confused and terrified but he started to run. His hand was a bleeding mess, his heart was racing, his mind was spinning but maybe he *could* really escape. Why was Devon Stone doing this? What was his endgame?

Devon Stone and Drew Devereaux just stood back in silence and watched him run.

Clovis James was waiting. He had watched the action from a short distance, and began his car engine, putting it into gear.

Panicked beyond rationality and still partially blinded by the strange flashing strobe, Darrin Rand never even saw the car approaching until it was too late.

The ravens, after swooping noisily back and forth in the grey skies, finally settled back into the treetops.

49

No, Darrin Rand did not die that morning.

His death had not actually been the intent even though Clovis James wanted to keep rolling his car back and forth over the little man until he was just a puddle of blood and broken bones.

It had been a well-coordinated effort right from the beginning.

Chester Davenport and Fiona Thayer had first spotted and then kept their eyes on Darrin Rand's car parked down the street from Devon's house. While Rand had taunted Richard Fleming just before killing him about not being able to drive the assassin's two Maseratis, Rand actually *did* have a car that he was very capable of driving. A Morris Minor, a small, very popular car at the time and seen everywhere. Even so, the vehicle had been retrofitted with special blocks so that Rand's short legs could reach the gas, brake and clutch pedals. Along with a few different counterfeit passports, he also possessed just as many fake drivers' licenses.

It must have frustrated Rand when Devon Stone didn't leave his house for days on end.

When the plan had been agreed upon, and Devon had left his house heading toward Hampstead Heath, Fiona cautiously followed Darrin Rand as *he* followed Devon. Rand never thought of looking behind him.

Fiona, herself a crack shot and assassin because of her MI5

involvement during the war, would have taken Rand down if he had been successful in shooting Devon Stone.

Clovis James's car, however, had severely shattered both of Darrin Rand's legs. The possibilities of him ever walking again were nonexistent.

Between the investigations of Scotland Yard and INTERPOL, the two homes of the assassin hired by Darrin Rand, Richard Fleming, had been located. The number and types of bizarre weapons found in each stunned the officers.

One month later Devon Stone stood over the bed of a bandaged Darrin Rand. Having been committed to Holloway Sanatorium, twenty-two miles outside of London in Surrey, the little man would be heavily sedated and restrained there for the rest of his life.

Neither said a word to each other.

———————⟫●⟪———————

Although there would be no way of finding out at this point, the probability of the children sired by Darrin Rand on his raping rampage throughout Germany during the war being born with the same affliction as him, achondroplasia, was 50%.

50

Three weeks later Devon Stone was hosting one of his infamous cocktail parties. He hadn't seen or even spoken to many of his friends for months. He felt that it was time...long overdue time... for one of his notorious bacchanals.

He hired three barmen along with a dozen servers for this event and even had the food catered. It was time for him to relax and simply enjoy himself for a while. A jazz trio was playing in his front parlor.

And by nine P.M. the place was jumping!

Amaryllis Cormier, following Devon's request, had brought Winston as her plus one. The overly friendly dog made the rounds, greeting the guests with tail wags and a big smile. Within the hour word of Winston's heroism had spread and he had a year's worth of belly-rubs and ear ruffling.

"Devon!" Amy said excitedly, when she finally tracked him down amongst the throng, "Fiona just told me all about the big showdown with that dwarf guy. You sure were taking one heck of a chance, weren't you? You were being foolhardy, if you ask me. Which, of course, you didn't."

Devon Stone laughed.

"It was a risk I had to take, young lady. Just like horse racing, I suppose. You win some, you lose some. Fortunately I didn't end up flat on the ground like my horse at the Grand National."

"You're being *way* too flippant about it, that's all I can say. And that's all I *will* say."

And she started walking away, heading toward where the bar had been set up.

"No, wait," she said abruptly turning around. "Just suppose let's say, somehow that little freak gets out again. Aren't you still walking around with a target on your back?"

"I probably *would* have had a target on my back, Amy, if certain circumstances were different. Aside from both his legs now being non-working, and both hands practically worthless, his violent ranting and raving when the sedatives wore off caused him to have a massive cerebral aneurysm. It ruptured two days ago. He'll possibly survive…or not. But at this point he has absolutely no idea what year it is, who he is, or where he is."

Devon grew pensive for a brief moment.

"Strange as it may seem, Amy, and it frightens me to even think this, much less say it. I actually sort of feel sorry for the little guy. He was dealt a lousy hand right from the day he was born. He could never overcome it, unfortunately. I doubt that he even tried. I wonder if that man was ever happy, even once, in his entire life."

Devon Stone sighed deeply and let a smile come back to his face.

"Come on, Amy. Have fun tonight. Shall I escort you to the bar?"

Devon Stone then escorted Drew Devereaux around the party, proudly introducing her to all of his friends, some of whom already knew her…or *about* her…from her photo exhibition. She looked stunning and Devon told her so often throughout the evening. It was apparent to everyone that Drew Devereaux held a very special place in Devon's heart. Something they had never seen before. DeeDee enthralled Devon's friends with story after story about the war, although her sharpshooting talent (with a rifle) was never discussed.

By eleven P.M. the place was still jumping, but with a houseful of laughing, babbling drunks. Actually, there were at least a dozen people that Devon had never seen before in his life. He didn't mind as long as they had fun, didn't break anything, steal anything, or kill anyone.

By two A.M. the party was finally dwindling down. The food was gone and Devon had made the rounds, catching up with all the friends he hadn't seen in months. He finally had a chance to chat with Maude Landis. Her son, Christian…Devon's publisher…had passed out drunk two hours earlier and had been carried upstairs to one of Devon's guest rooms.

"Devon, dear boy," Maude said grabbing him by the arm. If she had been wearing pearls she would have been clutching them to her chest. "I was just told by a few others about your recent, how shall I say it, escapade! Frightening! What in *heaven's* name were you thinking? You could have been killed."

She took a large gulp of her gin and stifled a slight drunken burp.

Devon just smiled and shrugged.

"But I wasn't. That all that matters, right?"

Chester Davenport slowly walked up behind the blathering lady and smiled at Devon. He made a silly face and it was all Devon could do to refrain from laughing in the poor woman's face.

"I was talking to that rude critic friend of yours a while ago. Is he still here?" Maude asked.

She glanced around quickly. Devon shook his head.

"I doubt very much that he's left yet. He's almost always one of the last to leave. I'm sure he is around here somewhere. Why?"

"Well, I doubt that someone like *him* partakes in anything like *your* escapades but I was talking to him about plays, musicals and murders. Agatha Christie has written several wonderful murder mystery *plays*, but they don't seem to make any musicals about murder mysteries now, do they? Isn't that strange?"

Devon didn't know where Maude was going with this, aside from the fact that she was probably drunk as a lord and slurring her words.

"But, wait…you know?" she continued. "There *was* one here at the West End last year, wasn't there?"

"I'm not really fond of musicals, Maude," he said.

He was politely trying to extract himself from her presence. He started to slowly back away.

"Yes, there *was*. And it was a jolly good one, at that. Several murders in it. Funny murders. I found it hilarious. And I never guessed who the killer was! It starred that American actress. Oh, what *was* her name? Veronica Barron! Yes, that was it! Veronica Barron. Perhaps you've heard of her?"

"Perhaps," smiled Devon Stone as he winked at Chester Davenport. "Perhaps I have."

By five A.M. the house was once again quiet. The guests had long since departed. The caterers had cleaned up and gone. The barmen had left one unopened bottle of Dom Pérignon Brut sitting in a still-cold ice bucket and Devon Stone was about to uncork it. He did so and carried it and two glasses up to his bedroom.

Drew Devereaux smiled as he entered the room. She sat up in the bed, drawing the sheets up around her, shielding her naked body.

"Are you going to propose a toast, Devon?" she asked with a wicked smile as she watched him approach the bed.

Devon put the bottle and glasses down for a moment on the nightstand as he slowly started to undress.

"Oh, DeeDee, I'm going to propose more than that."

"I've never been served champagne by a naked man before. You certainly know how to top off a great party, Devon."

Devon Stone laughed.

"Now…as for that proposal," he said as he raised his glass and offered one to her. "How does St. Tropez sound?"

"For what? And when?"

"For a honeymoon. And tonight."

Drew Devereaux downed her glass of champagne and let the sheets fall away from her body.

"Let's elope," said Devon Stone. "Today. Tonight."

Without even a moment's hesitation she leaped from the bed.

"Why not right now?" Drew said as she quickly ran to embrace him. "Let's go!"

EPILOGUE

Three Months Later: After an unguarded and unsupervised play date, Amy's dog Winston sired a litter of puppies with a neighbor's prize-winning Standard Poodle. The neighbor was furious, to say the least, but the puppies were extremely cute. Amy presented one of the female pups to Devon Stone, who had never owned a dog in his life. He fell in love with her on first sight and called her Winnie.

Four Months Later: Christian de Lindsay, having decided to leave the publishing business for something less taxing, opened an interior design studio financed by his mother, saint that she was. Within the year it would be shuttered.

Five Months Later: Amaryllis Cormier, bidding her job at The Poisoned Quill goodbye, bought a vacant building and opened a new floral shop on fashionable King's Road in Chelsea. The name of the shop, *Kiss My Aster*, generated smiles and laughter, easily lured customers in. The shop flourished.

Six Months Later: After a tempestuous on again/off again, dance-around courtship, Clovis James proposed to Maude Landis. Devon Stone warned his friend that all of Maude's three previous husbands had died, possibly as a means of escape.

One Year Later: At the age of fifty-two, Devon Stone became a father for the first time. He and his wife, Drew, named their beautiful baby daughter Danielle Bourke. He then decided to abandon murder and mayhem to start writing children's books from that point on.

Forgoing his pen name once and for all and reverting back to his given name of Daniel Stein, much to his surprise and delight, his very first book in that genre became an instant best seller. *Little Lucie Goosey* was about the adventures of a precocious, inquisitive gosling and her best friend, a little brown puppy by the name of Winston. Eventually it was turned into a long-running animated television series beloved by just about every child in the United Kingdom.

AUTHOR'S NOTES
(FACTS VS. FICTION)

Some of my astute readers may have picked up that I based my character Drew Devereaux on the famous American photographer and photojournalist Margaret Bourke-White. During World War II she was the first known female war correspondent as well as the first woman to be allowed to work in combat zones. Her countless hundreds, possibly even thousands of her photographs are world famous, including the ones published in *LIFE* Magazine taken during World War II and the Korean War.

She had narrowly escaped so many life-threatening incidents that the staff at *LIFE* Magazine dubbed her as "Maggie the Indestructible".

Although I have softened her persona for my character DeeDee, according to an editor of a collection of Bourke-White's photos she was regarded as imperious, calculating, and insensitive.

And, like the fictitious Drew Devereaux, Margaret Bourke-White met, fell in love with, and married a novelist: Erskine Caldwell. Unfortunately, though, they didn't live happily ever after. When the photographer headed off into World War II to take pictures, the author divorced her. He expected her to stay home, evidently, and prepare his meals.

And, as a side note, Barbra Streisand had wanted to make a film about Margaret Bourke-White but it never got the backing that she needed.

For more detailed info, you might want to Google that fascinating photographer.

I have taken a few liberties (artistic license if you will) with the notorious section of London encompassing Dorset/Duval Street. That, too, has a seedy past that deserves another trip to Google for more detailed (and accurate) information.

Regarding the very brief mention by Drew Devereaux in this book of the B-47 that went missing over the Mediterranean Sea on March 10, 1956. It really happened. A nuclear detonation was not possible because only two capsules of nuclear weapons material were in carrying cases. There was never an explanation for the disappearance nor was there ever any evidence found of the aircraft, its weapons or its crew.

Believe it or not, that surprising and shocking incident at the 1956 running of the Grand National actually *did* happen. Devon Loch, the horse owned by Queen Elizabeth The Queen Mother, had cleared the final fence and was certainly well in the leading position. He was forty yards from certain victory when he suddenly, and inexplicably, half-jumped into the air and belly-flopped down onto the turf. He wasn't injured, he got back up and finished the race far behind. There has never been an explanation for that odd behavior. It has been said that horses win races with their heads. But what had Devon Loch been thinking?

The Queen Mother was then quoted as simply remarking "Oh, that's racing!"

The incident became a part of the folklore of the event. In modern language the phrase "To do a Devon Loch" is used to describe snatching a last-minute failure from the jaws of victory.

The Grand National is considered one of the most dangerous horse races in the world because of the size of its fences, which range in height from 4'6" to 5'2", with some of the fences having a steep drop, a lower landing side than the take off side.

Had Devon Loch actually won the race he may have set a new record for the fastest finishing time, which the winning horse, ESB, missed by only four-fifths of a second. As for ESB, the gelding's unusual name? I'm thinking that perhaps it's because his dam's name was English Summer and his sire's name was Bidar.

Oh, yes. And about the Queen Mother's jockey, Dick Francis, on that fateful day. Following a long successful career as a winning jockey but eventually suffering a serious injury, he went on to become a beloved author of more than forty international best-selling murder mysteries, mostly based around horses and horse racing.

During World War II he had served in the RAF piloting fighter and bombing aircraft.

He had a long life (89 years) just as colorful as all the silks he wore as a jockey.

To all you chemistry majors out there, ketamine, the drug used by Richard Fleming to dull Judge Rathbun's senses before screwing him to death in this book wasn't invented/discovered until 1962. By the way, deaths by corkscrew and by an umbrella injecting mercury were methods used in actual murder cases.

As outlandish and far-fetched as it may seem in this book, Hitler's crazed plan to populate newly invaded lands with loyal Aryan citizens actually existed. I did *not* make it up. The German population had been declining. Propaganda programs were ordered to encourage German women to give birth. Often. Under the Third Reich, women and girls, some as young as fifteen, were told that it was their *duty* to give birth to as many children as possible, married or otherwise. Contraception was verboten. Free love reined! Mother's Cross medals and incentives were handed out profusely. Via the Propaganda Minister, Joseph Goebbels, magazines, posters, and pornographic films promoting "healthy eroticism" were produced.

As the war dragged on and on however, eventually the policy of Lebensraum (Living space) began to backfire. German women worn out from too many children at home began to seek illegal abortions.

My wife and I spent a few days in the wonderful city of London and then a week driving through the lush, beautiful countryside of Scotland back in 2005. London is an amazing city, great for just walking around, and one of our favorite places.

Scotland offered so many gorgeous vistas and castles for exploring. We stayed at the family-owned castle estate of Kilconquhar, dating back to the 16th century. It was nowhere nearly as plush as the Witchery Hotel in Edinburgh where Devon Stone stayed, but I used "our" castle as the model for the home of the corrupt, doomed Judge Rathbun prior to his death by corkscrew in this book, *The Murder Of Devon Stone*.

Using the unique Kilconquhar Castle for the home of one of my characters brought back some wonderful memories of the place. The dining room that was located in the large room by that turret to the left served exquisite breakfasts with the best pancakes I had ever eaten. And their roasts with locally grown vegetables served at dinnertime were exceptional.

A little history about the castle: Records of the castle go back to 1200 A.D. when it belonged to the Earls of Fife. In 1270, Adam, Earl of Fife, died on a crusade and his widow then married Robert de Brus, who became Earl of Carrick and Lord of Kilconquhar. Their son was Robert the Bruce.

Edinburgh Castle and the Royal Mile made the perfect locale for the first clash between Devon Stone and Darrin Rand. Someone's hand, forcefully stomped down upon on the rough cobblestoned Royal Mile, would easily have been smashed.

We stopped to explore several other castles as we drove around the small country. Their surrounding grounds are still beautifully maintained.

The Flying Scotsman, the train on which Devon Stone traveled from London to Edinburgh is now considered one of the most famous locomotives in the world.

The interior of one of its cars was quite luxurious as you can tell by the photo below. That's where Devon Stone did his writing and drinking while traveling to Edinburgh.

ACKNOWLEDGEMENTS

First and foremost I must again give thanks to my oldest grandson, Devon Stone Hasbrouck, for allowing me to use part of his name for my favorite character. He neither looks nor acts like my fictitious author although he *does* have a killer wit. Sarcasm seems to run in our family.

I offer a tremendous amount of gratitude to my loyal readers (most of them, probably, my family) and to the few book clubs to which I have been invited to speak. The fact that my books have encouraged many of my readers to do further research on all the tidbits of history that I impart makes me proud. My goal is to write entertaining, albeit light reading while also teaching things along the way. I do a lot of research as I write these tomes and I discover facts and words that amaze me. It gives me pleasure to pass those along.

How many times did *you* scramble to GOOGLE while reading this book?

And, as always, I save the absolute <u>best</u> for last. Six books ago (before this one) I promised my dear wife Gaylin, saint that she is, that "Horse Scents" would be my one and only folly. It was a whim that couldn't be denied. That being said, Devon Stone and I share two things in common: our love for gin & tonics, and writing, especially murder mysteries. One is affection and one is addiction.

Thank you, my dear patient, and sometimes-understanding wife, Gaylin, for nearly sixty years of marriage. Some tears through the years, but mostly a glorious time filled with adventures enjoyed all around our globe. Our two wonderful sons, Gregory and Christopher, have made us both incredibly proud. Somehow, despite my shenanigans along the way, they have grown into decent, successful men raising their own children to be decent, intelligent individuals.

Devon Stone Hasbrouck, Alexis Morgan Hasbrouck, Peyton Chase Hasbrouck, and Jacob Everett Hasbrouck (Jake, aka Hazzy) I love you more than you'll ever know!

But will there ever be another Devon Stone thriller in the future? No.

Printed in the United States
by Baker & Taylor Publisher Services

Printed in the United States
by Baker & Taylor Publisher Services